UNICORN'S INSTINCT

LARGE PRINT EDITION

A DAY CARE FOR SHIFTERS
BOOK THREE

ELVA BIRCH

For my dad.
Because every day is treasured.

CONTENTS

PREFACE

This is a crying book.

It is also cute and funny and full of love and hope and mercy, but bring tissues because it made my editor bawl and laugh in the very same paragraph. It has topics of mortality and sacrifice and fate, and examines what we can do with the life that we have.

(It also has a very cute puppy.)

CHAPTER 1

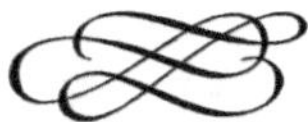

How much?

It was always the first question Becket asked when he arrived on the scene of an accident and started triage. What would this cost him? How much could he spare? Was it worth metering out the magic he had, or should he hoard it against a greater future injury? People could usually heal on their own, if he was willing to let them suffer.

The man who lay limp at the side of the road in the woman's arms didn't look hurt, but Becket could feel the weak force of his life, the agony and exhaustion. Becket was as puzzled as his teammates by the couple's sudden appearance through the smoke, and the just-as-sudden cessation of all the wildfire in a twenty-mile radius, though he'd at least had the advantage of *feeling* the wave of magic that swept the area.

The man made Becket's instinct tingle. The woman was only human, but the man she was holding was a shifter...and something else? Something capable of fire suppression on a scope that Becket had never seen before. And he wasn't particularly skilled at it, Becket thought, because he'd exerted himself to his absolute limits, and his life itself was now barely clinging to his human shell. He'd nearly burned out his mind altogether.

How much? he asked again.

His unicorn considered, casting ahead in time. *Not much*, it finally said. *If you are careful, and only give him a little shock, it might only be a few moments.*

Without it?

His unicorn hesitated. *I can't tell. He might find his way back. He might not. It would take a long time.*

How much would he miss a minute of his own life to assure someone else's?

Becket exchanged a look with the fire chief and nodded. Thomas stood and started directing the rest of the crew out of the way.

When he was sure that no one would see, he put his hand to the man's chest and let a tiny sliver of his unicorn's magic out, like a sharp blade slicing straight through into his heart. It was just enough to jolt him back together.

Their joyful lover's reunion was reward enough, Becket thought, when the man opened bleary eyes and tried to speak her name, Olivia.

He gave them one of his contact cards and, once they'd recovered enough, released them to stagger back to their car and go home. He wasn't sure what their story was, but shifters stuck together, when they could, and he knew that finding shifter-specific medical help was always challenging. They tended to ping alarm levels in some categories when bloodwork was taken, simulating the results of infection and cancer when none was present, and it was hard to hide their ability to heal and resist illness from a doctor who was investigating closely.

"Any trouble?" Thomas asked when he returned with the rest of the crew. They had confirmed that the fire was miraculously out, and that the road could be opened again.

"They should be fine," Becket said. Thomas wasn't a shifter, and he only knew that Becket's ability to heal people bordered on miraculous; he didn't know what it cost him.

In this case, it was just enough to take a minute off of Becket's life.

It was like having a fingertip shaved off with something so sharp and swift that it forgot to hurt. He knew it was gone, at some level, and he felt wrong for a moment, but he wouldn't really feel the pain of it.

Not until the end, which galloped closer every time he used the magic.

When he was young and indestructible, he was careless with the use. What was a minute here, or a few there? He could *save lives*. He used it on every window-hit bird and wing-crumpled butterfly that he ran across, sealing up cuts and soothing pulled muscles.

Then he realized what mortality was, and learned about morality at the same time, and learned to ration his gift and work to supplement it with actual medical knowledge. Healing with modern medicine may not be quite as rewarding, but it was considerably more sustainable.

He had settled into a footloose life, spending winters as a traveling pediatrician and summers as an EMT with forestry.

Becket enjoyed the life he'd won for himself. He made friends easily. He liked to travel. He felt useful.

"We're going to miss you this fall when you retire to the cushy life of an office doctor again,"

Thomas said, as they packed everything back up into the truck.

"I'm sure you can find someone else to put bandaids over the blisters that the crew get from wearing crappy socks," Becket said wryly.

He swung up into the truck and the conversation died to nothing over the rattle of the truck on the gravel road.

His next assignment was nearby, in the sleepy historical town of Nickel City, and he wasn't sure what he was going to do with an entire winter there. He thought wistfully of how Ian and Olivia had looked at each other but he knew better than to wish for a mate.

How could he want a mate, knowing he would die and leave them so soon?

CHAPTER 2

"Tara, are you done eating?" Vivian asked, hopping in on one foot as she tried to pull on her shoe and finger-comb her hair at the same time. Shane had wanted to nurse much longer than usual that morning, and mornings were already made of tight scheduling and too many things to do for the time that she had. She wasn't sure she'd gotten all of the conditioner rinsed out of her hair during her stolen two-minute shower. "We have to go, I can't be late!"

If they left in the next five minutes, it would give them ten minutes to get to the day care, she had to plan on five minutes there to get Tara and Shane checked in, if she could find a parking space close, then she had to get the paperwork for the insurance company notarized at the bank before her shift at the clinic. The bank opened at ten, her shift started at ten-thirty. If she could be there when they opened, if she caught all the traffic lights right, she ought to be able to just make it...

"Tara, where are you? You've barely touched your breakfast, why aren't you eating it?"

Tara's kirin head popped up from underneath her chair and Shane, strapped into his high chair, cackled in glee. Tara tipped her deer- and dragon-like face and her whiskers trailed after her.

Vivian had not entirely gotten used to Tara's new level of comfort with her shift form. Even though she'd known about them for a few years now, shifters as a whole were still a bit of a wonder. "Tara, honey, not at the breakfast table! I know you're the kirin who could, but could you *not* right now?"

As swift as thought, Tara was a little girl again, remorseful and guilty. "I dropped my egg," she explained, holding a tiny piece of fried egg aloft. "Sowwy, Mommy."

"I know you are," Vivian said, reining back her frustration with effort. Tara was at a sensitive age where she took everything really personally.

"Let's eat as much as we can as quickly as possible," she said encouragingly. "I'll get Shane ready."

Shane was just starting his adventures in solid food and he was gumming on his rice teething cake with drooly interest but he hadn't eaten much of it. "Can I have that for a minute, Baby? Just for a minute? I'll give it back."

Shane stared at her with uncertain eyes. Vivian tried to distract him and slip the cracker-shaped food from his fist. He grabbed it harder and began to cry. "Alright, we'll strap you both in," Vivian said, giving up on her plan to keep the cake from disintegrating in the car seat with him.

Still convinced she was going to steal his precious food and possibly that she was instituting some form of elaborate torture, Shane fought against being buckled into the car seat with considerable strength for his age and cried in protest. Vivian kissed his forehead and smoothed his jumper underneath the straps. "Someday, you'll forgive me for all the terrible torment I put you through. I hope."

He cried disconsolately.

Tara hadn't eaten anything else in the time that Vivian had gotten Shane ready and she was achingly aware of the hands of the clock above the sink, tapping steadily to *too-late* in the morning.

"We're just going to have to take it to go," Vivian said, sweeping it all into a zip-shut baggy. Tara protested because she hated to have her food mixed up in one bag, which is when Vivian realized that she hadn't packed a lunch for her daughter yet. A frantic search of the kitchen turned up a hastily-peeled carrot, a single-serve yogurt, and a three-pack of cookies. "I am the worst mother in the history of the world," Vivian muttered under her breath, rifling through the junk drawer for a plastic spoon.

Unfortunately, Tara heard her. "You're not worst, Mommy!" the little girl hastened to assure her and Vivian was not going to rush through a big hug, even if she wasn't sure whose comfort it was really for when she knelt down to get it.

Shane's crying changed in tenor and Tara ran to find him a selection of his favorite stuffies to distract him while Vivian finished packing what passed for a lunch.

"We're going to get a puppy," Tara was telling Shane comfortingly. "It's going to be a yellow puppy wif floppy ears."

"We're not getting a puppy," Vivian told her

daughter with a sigh. "I don't have time to take care of a puppy."

Time seemed to be her constant theme, and not enough of it.

There was still a chance to make it to the bank before work as she finished getting everything together.

But there were no parking spaces in front of the day care, or for two blocks in either direction. Vivian finally pulled up tight into half a spot, the back of her car almost blocking a fire hydrant, and herded Tara down the street with Shane in the car seat over one arm cutting off her circulation.

Tiny Paws Day Care looked unassuming from the street, with its old Saloon sign above the door. Vivian was buzzed in and Teacher Addy cheerfully met her to take Shane while Vivian coaxed Tara to take her shoes off a little more quickly, please.

In a stroke of mercy, there was no ticket on her windshield when she finally got back to the car, but all of the delays meant that she had no chance before her shift at the clinic to stop at the bank with her paperwork. As it was, she was scrambling in the back door about five minutes late, thinking regretfully of mornings in the past when she could breeze in ten minutes early to enjoy a leisurely cup of coffee and gossip with Crystal before getting started on the day's work.

"I'm here, I'm here," Vivian said, pausing at the sink to give her hands the fastest sanitizing wash in the history of the world. Did the birthday song still count if you sang it in your head at double speed?

Crystal reached around her to grab a clipboard hanging on the wall. "The new temporary pediatrician is here, and whew, boy, if you are not ready to date yet, I am going to ditch my family and have myself a wild affair because he is *ready to ride.*" She fanned herself with the clipboard suggestively.

Vivian had to stare at Crystal in surprise and a little horror. Crystal was absolutely not going to risk her family for a fling with the new doctor, but what really drew Vivian up short was—"Date? I can't date."

Jin had only been gone for a year and his death had left her with a pile of bills and a heart full of grief, pregnant and trying to raise a three-year-old daughter who could change into a Chinese unicorn. She was lucky enough now to have access to a day care that was designed to handle shifter children and generous about irregular payments, but it didn't feel much like luck the way she scrambled endlessly between her job and trying to be a mother, never getting enough sleep, working desperately to make her time and money stretch further than it ought to.

She didn't have anything *left* for dating. "Help yourself to the hot new guy," she said with a regretful sigh. "I've got my hands too full with the kids."

She couldn't tell Crystal about the shifting part, of course. Shifters were a well-kept secret, and keeping that secret was one of the many weights on her shoulders. What if someone found out about Tara and tried to take her away? Was Shane going to be a shifter? Jin said that shifters recognized each other, but Vivian was only human, so she had to assume *everyone* was a risk.

"He's a *pediatrician*," Crystal reminded her. "He'll understand about kids. Doctor Jamison is already talking about trying to extend his contract. He works summers as an EMT with the fire service. He even brought homemade cookies because it's his first day." The clinic had been searching for a doctor for several years now, since their previous pediatrician had retired and moved to Florida. They had been settling for temporary hires of traveling doctors while they continued to advertise for something permanent.

"He sounds like a unicorn," Vivian said, even knowing that Crystal wouldn't understand the depth of the irony. Jin had been an *actual* unicorn, something he'd kept close to his chest until Tara had been born. Vivian waited for the pang of grief that inevitably came from thinking about him, but she must be more tired than she realized because it was only the faintest of pains. She was also starving; she had never grabbed breakfast for herself that morning, trying to get food into the kids. "Cookies, you say?"

"In the break room," Crystal said. "Oh, it looks like we've got the Thompson triplets coming in today. I wonder what body parts they've broken now. Talk about a trial by fire. Your unicorn is going to have his hands full with his first patients."

"He's not my unicorn," Vivian said sharply, but Crystal was gone.

She didn't want to faint taking the vitals of her very first patients of the day, so Vivian headed for the break room. She might have a dollar in her purse to get an overpriced stick of salty beef jerky or a bag of chips from the vending machine.

She smelled the cookies even before she got into the break room: chocolate and cinnamon. Crystal had said that the new guy brought cookies, but she hadn't said that it was a giant platter with six different kinds of decadent fresh cookies: chocolate chip, chocolate crinkles, cinnamon snickerdoodles, gingerbread, oatmeal raisin, and —thoughtfully in a separate basket in case of allergies—peanut butter. Vivian looked longingly at the sweeter choices and opted for one of the protein-packed peanut butter cookies. Probably two would be alright. Three might look greedy, even if she was breastfeeding.

She was biting into her second, trying to savor it instead of wolfing it down frantically with her eyes closed, when someone behind her cleared their throat.

The cookie snapped in half in her hand and Vivian had to scramble to catch both halves, knowing that she looked ridiculous and clumsy as she turned and nearly choked on what she had in her mouth.

Crystal hadn't been kidding.

The new pediatrics doctor was absolutely gorgeous. *Ready to ride,* she'd said, and Vivian could see why. The guy was a page straight out of GQ, with dark hair, a beautifully-groomed beard, and a perfect, white-toothed grin. Pale gray eyes were almost silvery in his face.

"Good cookies," Vivian managed to say when she figured out how to swallow again. She hadn't reacted to anyone like this since...she balked at finishing the thought. He looked like a movie star. The one who did Sherlock Holmes and super-heroes. He was also wearing a smock that was covered in tiny teddy bears in top hats.

"I'm glad you like them," he said, and even his voice was perfect, smooth and rich, with the tiniest touch of a Boston accent. "Instinct told me I should bring them in today…"

CHAPTER 3

When Becket saw that his nurse would be Vivian Yang, he immediately formed an impression of a short Asian woman in his mind, and when the clinic assistant, Crystal, told him that she was very, very good at what she did and took no prisoners, he aged her up in his imagination to a gray-haired elder.

But Vivian Yang looked like a young, Midwestern cowgirl, with honey-highlighted brown hair, Swedish features, and breasts like state fair prize-winning watermelons straining under her smock.

He told himself firmly not to stare, and then she turned around with cookies shoved haphazardly into her mouth and it wasn't just her mammaries that arrested him.

Told you we should bring cookies, his unicorn nickered in satisfaction.

She had cornflower blue eyes in a sun-kissed face, a dust of freckles over her skin that was strongest on her nose.

"Good cookies," she said faintly around her mouthful, and Becket felt like sunlight had just come out from behind a cloud.

"I'm glad you like them," Becket stammered. "Instinct told me I should bring them in today."

Did her eyes narrow just the slightest bit in suspicion? She wasn't jangling like a shifter against his own instinct, but maybe she knew about them. Becket had been surprised how many people in the area had turned out to be shifters; Nickel City seemed to be crawling with them.

She swallowed and brushed self-consciously at her breasts where a few crumbs had collected. "I love the cinnamon kind," she said sheepishly, "but I thought I should have peanut butter for the protein. I'm always preaching about how breakfast is the most important meal, but I'm just awful at following my own advice."

Don't stare, don't stare, don't stare, Becket told

himself again. "I have the worst time listening to myself," he agreed. "I mean, I'm a doctor, so I know better, but there is nothing in the world like an entire tube of Pringles and a tub of ice cream for dinner."

Vivian's smile was slow and brilliant. "You are a doctor after my own heart!"

It was honestly hard to separate instinct from attraction from his unicorn's unexpected capering delight. She was beautiful and Becket's physical reaction to her was immediate, but she was also funny and her smile was contagious.

He wasn't entirely sure if she was flirting or only being friendly, and it was safest to assume the latter, but there was something about the flush in her cheeks that suggested she might be as interested in him as he was in her.

It was dangerous territory.

They were going to have to work together, and Becket didn't want to sabotage their professional relationship by grasping after something he shouldn't risk anyway. It wasn't that he didn't find the idea of a girlfriend for the winter appealing, but he wasn't even slightly willing to jeopardize his job.

So he forced himself to temper his smile. "I'm James Becket," he said, realizing that he hadn't actually introduced himself. "Everyone calls me Becket. Like a bucket. But with an E." This was not redeeming himself.

The Becket list, he thought wryly to himself.

"Vivian Yang." She gave her hand another brush on her thigh for peanut butter cookie crumbs before she shook his hand, and her handshake was bold and strong. If she was chagrinned to be caught stuffing herself with cookies, she was certainly covering it with professional cheer. "Let me know if you have any questions or need to know where anything is. Did Crystal go over our system with you?"

Becket made sure he let go of her hand well before he wanted to, and then worried that it looked too cold and brief. "Yes, she's got me all caught up. We used some of the same software at my last clinic, and if I get helplessly lost in this maze, I'll holler until someone finds me."

Her smile was sunshine again, just a hint of a blush on her cheeks, and even if Becket wasn't planning to pursue anything with her, it was nice that she clearly liked him. Maybe even *liked* liked him.

It was like he was thirteen again.

A really horny thirteen.

"I'm going to go get your first patients ready,"

she said merrily. "I'll send a search party if you aren't in the room in ten minutes."

Becket only remembered why he'd come into the break room after Vivian had left. Coffee. He was here for a cup of coffee, not a flirtatious encounter with a new professional contact. He just hadn't expected Vivian, or her tremendous breasts, and he was firm with himself that he needed to stop thinking about both of them immediately. All of them. HER. He needed to stop thinking about *her*.

Neither his will nor the coffee really helped, and when Crystal startled him as he was flipping through the charts, he nearly wore the latter.

"How do you like Vivian?" Crystal asked bluntly.

It took every ounce of Becket's self-control not to blurt, "Boobs!"

"She seems great," he managed to say, and he had a sneaking suspicion that *he* was blushing now. "Very competent. She said she'd send a search party if I got lost."

"Perfect!" Crystal said. "And just so we're completely clear, the coworker dating policy is that it's absolutely fine as long as it doesn't interfere with our jobs."

Becket eyed her. Was Crystal trying to hit on

him? She was an attractive older woman, with a pleasant smile and curly brown hair and her look was frankly appreciative. If Becket hadn't already met Vivian, he might have considered her in a carnal way—she was forward and funny and probably a pile of fun in the bed. But if a relationship with Vivian was complicated as his nurse, the power dynamic with Crystal as his receptionist was even more questionable, and it was Vivian that was making the fit of his pants problematic. "I…thank you. That's good to know?"

"You'll be needed in the pink room next," Crystal said, pointing at the chart in his hands. "We've color-coded everything, because it's way more fun that way."

"Thanks," Becket said, more sincerely. He gave his coffee cup a quick wash and left it in the drainer, which caused Crystal to fan herself in appreciation.

"Oh my God," he heard her murmur as he left, "he even washes dishes!"

He crossed paths with Vivian at the door to the pink room. "Pink! It's not just for girls!" she teased as they passed each other in the doorway. Becket had to suck himself back quite far to dodge her amazing cleavage, and it took a moment to get himself back on track to do his first exam.

The rest of the day, they passed like ships in the night, trading charts as they handed off clients, briefly comparing notes. Even if he hadn't been absolutely taken by her beauty and charm, her competency would have won his heart. She was completely professional, absolutely on point, and as smart as a whip, suggesting some things that he'd already come up with and several that he hadn't.

He knew that some doctors were threatened by talented nurses, but Becket was honestly overjoyed. He was going to love working here, and not just because the narrow back hallways made getting past each other a smiling, blushing, squeezing affair every time.

The patients loved her, and even her handwriting was perfect.

"That was your last one!" Crystal told him, as he handed over the final clipboard. "How was your first day?"

"As smooth as a first day has any right to be," Becket said gratefully. "It's clear you have a well-oiled machine here and I think I'll fit in well. Thank you so much for all of your help today."

Crystal preened happily. "I think you'll fit in just *fine*."

He was disappointed to see that Vivian's coat and boots were both gone. It wasn't really that he'd planned to linger over drawn out goodbyes, but he had somehow hoped for a little conversation that wasn't all work-related. Would it be too forward to ask her to show him around Nickel City?

He could not get Crystal's assertion that office romance would be happily accepted out of his mind.

Could be the one, his unicorn said wistfully.

But the reminder chilled Becket's ardor. This could be something short and fun, but it could never be anything more.

The one was completely out of the question.

CHAPTER 4

"Tara, you have to eat your food, honey. You'll be hungry when we get to Tiny Paws."

Tara was swinging her legs in boredom—she had already been sitting at the table for close to forty-five minutes and had only eaten a tiny fraction of her peanut butter toast. "It's dry," she complained.

Vivian reminded herself that there were pickier kids. Somewhere. Somehow. She felt like she ought to draw a hard line and make Tara eat the food she had, but she was also a veteran of many, many breakfast battles and knew when to fold. "Do you want some jam on it?" she offered desperately.

Tara considered the proposal and gravely nodded.

Vivian rattled through the fridge until she found the jam. "Mm," she said coaxingly. "It's strawberry."

Vivian smeared a thick layer of jam over the cold toast and took a bite herself to make it look more tempting. The jam was too sweet and the bread was dry, but Vivian was also absolutely starving, so it didn't really matter.

Tara took it back and nibbled half-heartedly at it while Vivian ransacked the fridge for a lunch for her.

The phone rang while she was trying to spread peanut butter that was too cold on bread that was too soft for a sandwich that Tara probably wouldn't eat anyway. "Vivian," she said, thumbing it on.

"Oh, Vivian, I'm so sorry."

Vivian's heart dropped. "Cherry?" This couldn't be good news.

"I can't take Tara and Shane until noon today. Addison called in sick and I'm short-handed until Shea comes in. I would risk taking them anyway, but Veronica Chase will be by this morning to look at some roof damage and I think she's hoping to catch me violating childcare laws."

Vivian rested her forehead on the cabinet above the counter. "Well, it's probably for the best that Addison doesn't come in sick," she said patiently. "Not all of the kids are shifters." If there was one blessing in Tara's shape-changing magic, it was that she never got ill. Shifter children could break limbs and skin knees like champions, but they healed fast and Tiny Paws was almost completely free of the usual day care snuffles and colds. Shane wasn't a shifter, though, and some of the other children had human siblings that attended.

"Thank you so much for understanding," Cherry said, her voice rich with relief.

Vivian wanted to protest that it wasn't fair, that she was desperate, that she was one of Cherry's first customers and didn't that earn her special consideration...? But she also knew that Cherry wouldn't cancel unless she absolutely had to.

Vivian didn't realize until after she'd hung up that it was quite unusual for Addison herself to be sick. She dismissed the worry and called Crystal. "I don't have childcare this morning," she said. "I can't come in until the afternoon."

"Oh, we need you, honey," Crystal said firmly.

"Bring the kids in, they can stay up front with me for the morning."

"Are you sure?" Vivian wasn't sure what she dreaded more—being a burden to Crystal, or the chaos that two small children could be. Even a girl as quiet and reserved as Tara was a lot to deal with, and Shane was a needy baby.

"Absolutely," Crystal assured her. "I've got crayons for Tara and a spot by my desk for Shane. I'm totally not getting enough baby time right now, and my kids have all declared that they have no interest in giving me grandbabies. You'll be doing me a favor. Or maybe you'll be doing my kids a favor. Either way, bring them in."

"You're the best, Crystal."

"I know!"

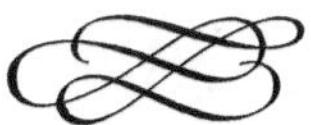

CHAPTER 5

Becket did not bring cookies in the next day, but when he found a little girl in his office, he wished that he had. He felt the jangle of instinct a mere moment before he found her.

"Hi," he said quietly.

She was hiding behind his filing cabinet, her knees pulled up to her chest. Becket didn't need instinct to tell him that she was shy, but it told him at once that she was a shifter. Something unusual, from the way that she made his skin shiver. He sat down on the floor opposite from her. "I'm Dr. Becket. Who are you?"

Her big dark eyes drilled into him suspiciously, then she seemed to relax. "Tara Yang," she said quietly. "I'm lucky."

She had wavy dark brown hair with long bangs, and a round face. Her eyes were startlingly blue. Was she Vivian Yang's daughter?

It suddenly occurred to Becket that Vivian might be married, and the idea caused a jolt of alarm. He hadn't looked for a ring and he probably should have before he spent a night lusting after her like a horny college student.

Horny, his unicorn snorted. For a creature of supposed grace and elegance, Becket's unicorn had a ridiculous love of puns and terrible jokes.

"Does your mom work here?" he guessed, and Tara nodded vigorously.

"Is her name Vivian?" Becket

Tara nodded again. "She helps people."

This was dangerous ground, Becket realized. Even if Vivian was divorced, Becket didn't need a relationship and he shouldn't be thinking about one at all. It wouldn't be fair to either of them. Or to the daughter she apparently had.

"I have a puppy," Tara told him confidently. "He's yellow with soft, fwoppy ears."

"He sounds really cute," Becket said. "What's his name?"

Tara's face scrunched up thoughtfully. "I don't know."

"That's a funny name for a dog," Becket teased her.

Tara stared at him for a moment and then dissolved into giggles. She was probably the cutest thing that he had ever seen in his life. "I'm hungwy," she said. "I was looking for the snack castle and got lost."

"Snack castle?"

Tara nodded vigorously. "It takes money. Mommy has money."

"The vending machine?" It was probably pretty impressive when you were two feet high.

Tara looked at him blankly and then nodded slowly.

"I bet your Mommy is looking for you right this moment," Becket said. "You want to help me find her?"

Tara looked steadily at him and then nodded, crawling carefully out from the narrow space between the filing cabinet and the wall. She was wearing a purple dress covered in flowers and butterflies over white tights with stained knees. She gave Becket her hand and Becket solemnly took it.

"Do you like cookies?" he asked, as they went out into the hallway.

"I like cookies!" Tara said happily. "My puppy likes cookies, too."

"I've lost your daughter," Crystal said cheerfully when Vivian returned to the nurse's station with the clipboards from her morning appointments. "Shane is happy, though!"

"Oh, well, one out of two isn't bad," Vivian said. "Hi, sweetie." Shane was gumming on a plastic cup. She'd brought a dozen Mensa-approved toys to entertain him, but it figured that he was most enamored of a disposable cup. He extracted the lip of the cup—now covered in drool—and waved it at her, beating it against his car seat, then seemed to notice it again like it was brand new. "Oh! Oh! Oh!" he hiccuped in joy.

"They're like little stoners, aren't they?"

Crystal observed. "'My hands are huuuuuge and everything is really interesting!'"

Vivian chuckled. "Where did you last see Tara?"

She wasn't *very* worried about her daughter; Tara was such a cautious child and was always asking for permission to do things. She wasn't prone to eating unknown things, climbing, or jumping. Vivian wasn't sure if it was just in her nature, if Vivian herself had been too strict as a parent, or if it was uncertainty because she'd lost her father so young, but she was confident that Tara hadn't gone far. There was no way for her to get out of the clinic without being seen.

"She was right there coloring," Crystal said, pointing to a little nest of toys and papers past her chair. "I was saying that we might go get a snack and then the phone rang. I swear, my eyes were only off of her for about three seconds. She hasn't been gone long at all."

"She probably went to look in the vending machine," Vivian guessed. "Hang on, Shane, I'll go find your big sister."

But she didn't have to go anywhere at all, because Doctor Cookies—Doctor Becket—himself showed up in the doorway holding Tara's hand.

If he'd been handsome the day before, he was

about a hundred times more when he was gazing adoringly down at Tara, who was smiling trustingly back up at him. And Tara didn't trust anyone.

Down girls, Vivian told her breasts as they came alive at the sight of him.

"My ovaries," Crystal whispered.

"I found the very charming Miss Tara Yang in my office just now and she tells me that she was looking for a snack and got lost."

You're the snack, Vivian thought and she had to bite her lip not to say it.

"He's the snack," Crystal whispered for her. "Oh my *God*, I said that out loud."

Vivian had not realized how sexy it was possible to look in a doctor's smock. This one was, if anything, more ridiculous than the last one he'd worn, with jungle animals in pastel colors all over it. Her whole body was reacting in totally inappropriate ways.

"Mommy! He's tingly!"

Vivian stepped on Crystal's foot before she could whisper anything with innuendo about tingling. Did Tara mean that he was a shifter? Or was instinct telling her something? She certainly didn't seem upset or afraid.

"Thank you so much for finding her," Vivian

managed to say, with mostly the correct syllables. She couldn't really look much above the collar of his smock because she was afraid of what would happen if she looked into his silvery eyes. "Tara, you aren't supposed to leave this room without a grown up."

Tara, who took it very personally when she did something wrong, wilted. "Sowwy," she said. "I was hungwy."

"We'll get you a snack," Vivian promised. To Becket's collar she explained, "I can't take them to the day care until noon because they are under-staffed today."

"No problem at all," Becket assured her. "Tara was telling me all about your new puppy." Then he added, "Them?"

Shane chose that moment to drop his new favorite cup and he gave a wail of angry protest and kicked his legs, rocking the car seat. "This is Shane," Vivian said, crouching to pick up his slimy cup. "Oh, let me wash this off before I give it back to you, honey."

"I'll do that," Crystal cried. "I have to go and splash cold water on my face anyway. Menopause! I'm in a volcano!"

She took the cup from Vivian and vanished down the hall.

Shane screwed up his face and looked like he was going to burst out into a full-out fit. Vivian swiftly unbuckled him. "Want to go for a little walk, young man?" she said, lifting him up into her arms fast enough to change his scream from angry to happy. "I don't think that the vending machine has disposable cups in it, but maybe you're up for some Goldfish after your first course." Her breasts felt heavy and she was keenly aware of their fullness. Vivian feared that was only partly due to Shane's proximity.

"I like Golfish!" Tara offered.

Vivian dared to look over at them. Tara was still clinging to his hand and Becket's face looked...conflicted. Was he mad because she'd brought her kids in? He'd said it was no problem, but maybe he was only being polite. That quenched her ardor considerably. But then he looked tenderly back down at Tara, and Vivian was afraid that she was going to start leaking right then and there. Why were bodies so inconvenient?

"I have a patient to go see right now," he explained to Tara. "I think your mom can get you a snack, now."

"Bye, Docker Becket!" Tara said cheerfully, releasing his hand to wave at him.

"Thank you for finding her," Vivian said hastily.

"Of course," he said, and then he was looking at her again, straight into her soul with those pale gray eyes. "I'm happy to. Any time."

"Great," Vivian said stupidly.

"Mommy, I want Golfish."

Vivian made herself swallow. "How do we ask for things?"

"Mommy, may-I-please give me Golfish now!"

Becket laughed, then seemed to cut it off abruptly. He opened his mouth to say something, then seemed to reconsider it, shook his head, and turned to leave, returning just a moment later to grab the next appointment clipboard from the station.

Then he was gone, and Vivian heard Crystal hail him in the hallway.

"They broke the mold with him," Crystal said, fanning herself appreciatively as she came back in. She appeared to have splashed literal cold water on her face, and she presented the cleaned and dried cup to Shane, who shrieked in joy, grabbed it, and promptly threw it down on the ground.

"At least this time it isn't coated with slobber to collect floor fuzzies," Vivian said as she crouched to pick it up. She gave it an experienced blow and decided it was good enough.

Shane held onto it this time, but decided that banging it against the side of Vivian's face was the most fun.

"Got a date yet?" Crystal wanted to know.

"No," Vivian said, reminding her breasts that they didn't. "Of course not. He looked a little freaked out."

"Oh my gosh, Viv, he probably thinks you're married. Did he see your fingers?"

"I don't know," Vivian said around the cup being drummed on her head. "They were kind of busy. Let's not do that with the cup, honey."

"Golfish, Mommy," Tara said more insistently. "I'm hungwy. I'm going to waits away."

"You're not going to *waste* away," Vivian told her, smiling anyway. "Come on, let's go get something from the vending machine."

* * *

CHERRY WAS DEEPLY apologetic when Vivian got Shane and Tara to Tiny Paws.

"I am so sorry I had to cancel this morning," she said. "But Veronica, she's looking for any reason to sink me." Cherry usually looked serene and cheerful, but Vivian thought she looked tired and discouraged this morning.

"Nickel City needs Tiny Paws," Vivian said. "And I don't know what I'd do without you."

Cherry's face soothed into a grateful smile. "Oh, honey!"

They exchanged a warm hug that Vivian held onto an extra moment. She genuinely wasn't sure what she'd have done without the shifter community that she'd found through Tiny Paws. It would have been impossible to arrange playdates or help Tara understand her shifter half without the day care, because she wasn't a shifter and had no idea who to trust. Cherry and her staff had helped Vivian understand her daughter's special needs and abilities.

To say nothing of the fact that she didn't know how else she would go to work and pay their bills. She trusted Crystal, but bringing the kids to the clinic was a stopgap at best. They'd taken more of her time than she wanted them to that day, and she could still feel what she suspected was Dr. Becket's disapproval—that wariness and extra distance that hadn't been there before.

Maybe having kids had just taken her out of the dating pool.

It seemed like he liked them, certainly he was amazing with them, but he'd been much chillier with her today than he had been the previous day.

When she rushed back to work, wondering why she was even still considering this guy as any kind of romantic possibility, he greeted her with a smile and a chart, and Vivian wondered if she'd imagined the coolness of the morning.

They fell into a perfect rhythm of work and service, balancing swift care with careful consideration and Vivian found herself falling for him all over again. He was just so good with the kids and so smart and thoughtful and kind.

Was she ready for this kind of thing? He was only there for the winter, was that a good thing, because she didn't have to worry about messing up a long term working relationship, or was it a terrible thing, because she'd let herself get too involved and then mourn what might have been?

How was she even considering dating, as full as her hands were with her kids?

"Let me get that for you!" Becket was a consummate gentleman, and Vivian was delighted but not terribly surprised when he hurried to open the door for her as she was leaving, her hands full of Tara's leftover things.

"I'm sorry again that I had to bring the kids in today," she said honestly.

"They were great," Becket said. "What kind of monster would I be if you couldn't bring in kids when childcare fell through? They were never in the way, and it wasn't any more chaotic because of them than it would have been anyway."

"I only lost one of them!" Vivian could not resist shooting him a glad and grateful look, only wondering afterwards if it wasn't a little on the besotted side. "Well, thanks for understanding."

"Can I get your car door?"

"Oh, thanks. I didn't realize that Tara had brought so much with her."

Vivian was able to unlock the door with her keyfob and Becket opened her passenger door so that she could dump Tara's toys into the seat.

He didn't immediately go to his own car, but waited while Vivian fished an escaping stuffy off the floor mat and shut the door.

"It might snow by the end of the week," Vivian said. "I hope you have a better coat."

He was wearing a windbreaker with no hood, just a shell. Vivian, in her wool coat, was still a little chilled.

"I have a winter coat," Becket said with a shrug. "But it seemed like a down coat was overkill for today and I don't have a lot in between."

"A sweater, then?" Vivian reminded herself that she didn't need to be mothering him. The doctor was perfectly capable of avoiding hypothermia without her meddling. And she definitely didn't need to offer to keep him warm. That would be utterly inappropriate.

"Words of wisdom," Becket agreed.

"I…have to go pick up my kids."

Neither of them made a move to go.

"You…probably should," he said at last.

Vivian didn't understand how anything so awkward could feel so…exciting. She was on a rollercoaster, sure that he was irritated with her, no, attracted to her, no, impressed by her, no afraid of her. She hadn't been this uncertain about her own feelings in an achingly long time.

One thing was sure, if she stood here forever, they'd both have hypothermia and no one would pick up Tara and Shane.

"Welcome to Nickel City," she finally said, and she forced herself to go around her car and get into it. She even remembered how to turn it on and drive away, although she backed up like she'd learned to drive at clown school because she was thinking too hard about how handsome he was.

CHAPTER 7

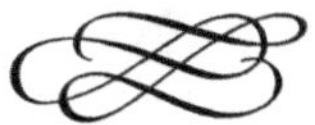

Sometimes, instinct was a real pain in the ass.

Why are we out here? Becket asked his unicorn. *Where are we going?*

October in Montana was not terribly warm. It was drizzling, and a little bit windy, and the combination was absolutely miserable.

His unicorn felt like a bloodhound in his head, pausing to snuffle at the air, then driving him in a beeline, first one direction, then another, and another, and…

Are we going in a circle? Can we please go home now?

The overpriced rental didn't really feel like home yet, but Becket kept telling himself he should unpack and maybe buy some cheap art so that it did. He hoped that his unicorn could get them back as unerringly as he was getting them nowhere.

Somewhere! was all that his unicorn would say. *Somewhere soon!*

There was a dead end ahead of them, the road stopping in a cul-de-sac with an abandoned house, an empty lot full of half-grown trees, and a utility corridor with No Trespassing signs. A car that had been idling at the end of it shifted into gear and sped out past them, driving Becket over to the side of the road and splashing cold mud up his legs at a pothole.

Jerk, he thought.

There, his unicorn said firmly, focused at the place where the car had been.

Do you need to shift or something? Becket asked. It was hard to be a horse-sized shifter with a glittering horn on his forehead in a suburban neighborhood; it had been a hot minute since they'd had a chance to discreetly get out so they could stretch their legs.

It was dark there, away from the last house lights, and Becket stumbled gracelessly over a fallen stick. The worn sidewalk had drifts of autumn leaves. It probably would have been a crunchy and delightful walk if it wasn't soggy and near freezing.

He was nearly ready to turn around and drag his irritating body companion back the way they'd come when he heard an unhappy yip.

There! his unicorn said.

Becket sighed and roamed further back into the woods at his unicorn's strident command.

The puppy—he was sure now that there was one—was pale in the dark shadows, and very small, tucked underneath an upside down shopping cart. At the sight of him, it gave an excited bark, and then settled into whining.

Becket lifted the cart easily, not sure if the puppy had been deliberately trapped underneath it, or if it had wiggled its way under and been unable to find its way out.

It was certainly wiggling now, its fluffy tail a metronome as it came bounding fearlessly out to greet Becket. It fell on its face no less than twice as Becket tipped the cart over on its side, barreling into Becket's leg. It was a golden retriever puppy, he guessed, fat and fuzzy and pale yellow, with soft floppy ears and soulful dark eyes. He was young. Becket didn't know much about puppies, but this one must be barely old enough to be away from its mother.

Had he been dumped here? Lost? Becket crouched down and the puppy flung himself up, trying to lick his face and scramble into his lap. Becket nearly fell over backwards at its tiny onslaught, and gathered it into his arms out of self defense. The puppy's whole body quivered in happiness and Becket was licked thoroughly as he stood up with him.

Well, he couldn't exactly leave the poor thing here. Maybe he should knock on a few nearby doors, he thought, and try to find his owners.

Assuming his owners hadn't left him on purpose.

Becket could honestly not imagine anyone wanting to get rid of such a joyful, sweet creature, but babies of all species could be a handful. He started to approach the nearest house, but his unicorn came alive and dragged him past. *Not there.*

It was another *not there* at the next house, and the next, until Becket was frustrated and it was starting to rain even harder. It was cold enough that it was nearly sleet.

Where, then?

He broke into a half-jog at his unicorn's insistence, and then they were over an entire block, approaching a small, cheerful one-level house with a fenced back yard.

Yang, the name on the mailbox read.

You have got to be kidding me, Becket said to his unicorn. But Tara had been telling him about her new yellow puppy. It *must* be theirs.

He hadn't been able to stop thinking about Vivian Yang since he'd left work. As his nurse, she was usually dealing with the patients before he got to them, and he could see her handiwork in how relaxed and ready they were, all their vitals carefully recorded, with neatly ordered notes that made his job a hundred times easier. She basically did all the heavy lifting for him, even offering little suggestions and highlights. *History of sepsis,* a sticky note reminded him on one case. *Probably pink eye - 3 siblings in day care* another filled him in. *Allergy to penicillin, has done well with amoxicillin,* another pointed out. Things he might have figured out, but didn't have to.

He watched her administer a vaccine, impressed by how well she handled the distraction of the young patient, and how sure her jab was.

He didn't mind giving her the credit she was due, but he knew that he shouldn't be thinking about how he'd like to jab *her,* even if Crystal had been agonizingly clear about the fact that there was no husband in the picture. (Did he know that Vivian was *single*? And also, in case he hadn't heard, it was amazing how completely *single* she was. Oh, had she mentioned that Vivian was *single*?)

Becket didn't want to come right out and ask why she had two young children on her own, though he was sure that Crystal would have been happy to tell him. Crystal seemed to have very few inhibitions on her tongue.

Because it didn't matter how single Vivian was. He had a looming expiration date and the last thing he needed was to fall in love with someone and break their heart.

CHAPTER 8

"Mommy, someone's at the door!"

Vivian had her hands full with a dirty diaper and she wasn't sure if Tara was playing pretend. There hadn't been a knock or a doorbell, and Tara's games were often based around *anything to make Mommy pay attention at the worst time.*

"Do you think it's a circus, coming to put my monkeys in a show?" Vivian asked. "Maybe it's a monster! Grrr!"

Tara giggled, and then vanished from the room.

Shane kicked his legs free, and Vivian had to try a second time to get his romper up over them. "Who's my wiggle-monster? Who's never still?"

Shane's latest milestone was unleashing a whole catalog of strange expressions. In quick succession, he tried out a toothy grin, a confused grimace, a wide-eyed look of shock, and a look of deep disgust. Vivian mimicked them back at him to the best of her ability, and he laughed and banged on the wall with his fist as she unbuckled him from the diaper table.

There was a knock at the door, and Vivian heard it creak open.

"Wait!" she called in alarm. "Tara, you can't just open the door for a stranger!"

But it wasn't a stranger, she discovered, as she bolted with Shane from the back hallway.

It was Doctor James Becket, soaking wet, holding an equally soaking wet ball of yellow fur on her porch.

"My puppy!" Tara yodeled. "He brought my puppy!"

"I found him out on an empty lot," he said sheepishly. "I was looking for his owners and I remembered Tara telling me about her new puppy."

"It's our puppy!" Tara said, dancing at his feet. She was rarely so animated. "Our puppy!"

"That's *not* our puppy," Vivian protested. "We don't have a dog. We're not *getting* a dog."

Tara was trying to pull him into the house and Vivian couldn't let him just stand out there in the rain, which was starting to blow in and puddle on the floor. "Come in, shut the door, and dry off," she said practically.

It was practical, wasn't it? It felt like the moment from a romance book, with a suitor making a grand gesture that was thwarted by weather itself. Except that romance books rarely had children gumming up the works. Babies came later, in convenient epilogues.

"I'm so sorry to bother you," Becket said, stepping in and shutting the door behind him. The puppy in his arms, wild-furred and wriggling, tried to escape, straining towards Tara, who was reaching up for him. Vivian was honestly not sure which of her unexpected guests looked more bedraggled and adorable.

"Go get a towel, Tara. Two towels, please. From the pile of grubby towels in the hall closet. Can you reach those?"

Tara scampered off to try, singing, "Puppy! Puppy! Puppy!"

She came back with two towels that she *could* reach, which turned out to be Vivian's best white towels, but she didn't want to be a grinch about it, so she merely handed them to Becket. He crouched down with Tara and one of the towels to dry the puppy, who shook himself vigorously as soon as his paws touched the ground…and nearly fell over at the uncoordinated effort of it.

Becket and Tara dried the puppy and he growled and wiggled and tried to chew on the towel and dropped over on his side waving his little paws in the air.

It was amazing how much he fluffed up, from a spiky-wet and bedraggled mess, to a sweet-faced puffy little dandelion. He had good manners, and although he chewed on fingers a few times, he had a gentle mouth and was affectionate and sweet. He licked Tara thoroughly and she squealed in joy.

Becket told them the story of his rescue as he stood and dried himself off with the other towel. He'd found the poor creature abandoned under a shopping cart, but he was evasive about why he'd been at the end of a dark cul-de-sac, poorly dressed for the rain in a thin windbreaker with no hood.

Vivian had her own suspicions regarding instinct, but she had enough to do juggling a squirming Shane and keeping her own wild libido in check. Becket was soaked beneath his jacket, and his thin T-shirt was molded to a body that was everything she'd imagined it would be underneath his doctor's smock.

"I could, ah, throw your shirt in the dryer for a few minutes," she offered, as he tried futilely to wring it out while it was still on him, only pulling it tighter over his shoulders. She realized that this was a terrible suggestion as soon as he took it off and she was struck completely dumb at the sight of his chest.

Down girls, she told her breasts, because she might not have a shifter's sense of instinct, but she was definitely *tingling* for this guy.

At least he didn't offer to take off his pants, as well, because Vivian suspected that her tenuous hold on civility would have been entirely lost. "I'll just toss this in with…oh dear…"

Tara handed her a filthy damp towel and Becket gave her a considerably cleaner one. Vivian didn't dare put Shane down in reach of the puppy, so she carried him with her to the laundry room off the kitchen.

There were already clothes in the dryer, from days ago, and Vivian had to pull them out, one-handed, in order to start the new load. She set the timer for ten minutes, hoping it would be enough to dry Becket's shirt but not set the stains in her towel. Probably, she shouldn't put the dirty towel in at all.

It was really hard to think around her unbelievable lust for the man that had just walked in like a lady's night runway model and taken off his shirt for her. Vivian squeezed Shane and reminded herself that she should definitely not read too much into any of this. He'd just rescued a puppy on a rainy October night, and that's all there was to it. He'd just rescued a puppy, and he baked cookies, and he was nice, funny, and gorgeous, and it had been a long, long time since she'd had feelings in her pants like this.

The timer from the kitchen startled her, and she scrambled to turn it off, putting Shane into his high chair with some cheerios before checking the lasagne in the oven.

"Do you want to join us for dinner?" she called, deciding that the frozen meal needed a few more minutes. The edges were bubbling, but the center looked suspiciously solid. "We have plenty!"

"It smells amazing," Becket said, appearing in the doorway to the kitchen. He was still brain-meltingly shirtless. "I'd love to, if it's no trouble." He said it with a certain amount of resignation, as if he'd just been bullied into it.

Vivian tried to analyze whether or not she'd sounded too pushy about it and decided she hadn't. "Tara will eat approximately two bites, I'll pull out a few noodles for Shane, and I couldn't possibly eat the rest of this myself. I'm usually sick of the leftovers within a few days, so you'll be doing me a favor. Hang on..."

Vivian sidled out past him, entirely too close for comfort, accidentally brushed him with her breasts despite her best attempts, and fled for her bedroom. She returned with her most oversized sweatshirt, a Shifting Sands Academy hoody from a fanclub she'd been a member of when she still had the time and energy to read for fun.

Becket gratefully put it on, and Vivian told herself she wasn't sorry that he did as the last of his delicious abs were covered. It didn't fit him particularly well, straining across the shoulders.

She also realized then that the kitchen table and chairs were half-drowning in cereal boxes and unsorted mail, a laundry basket full of clean but mismatched socks, electrical chargers, and insurance paperwork. She had a spot cleared at the end of the table that was just big enough for herself and Tara. "Oh, let me just clean this off, real quick. Would you keep an eye on Tara and our visitor?"

"Of course!" Becket politely retreated to the living room to sit with Tara and Vivian could hear them conversing about the puppy and finding toys that were safe for him to play with.

Everything went onto the counters, or the floor, or heaping higher on the remaining unused chairs. *When had it all gotten so out of control?* Vivian had to wonder, putting the most critical insurance paperwork by her phone.

Everything was roughly sorted and the space was usable by the time that the timer buzzed again. Vivian vowed to make the time to get it cleaned up for good very soon, because it felt so nice to have the entire kitchen table clear.

The lasagne looked much better this time, but was, of course, inedibly hot, so Vivian had a moment of respite to stand in the doorway and watch Becket play with her daughter.

The puppy was a bundle of energy, but Vivian was reassured both by how respectful Tara was being with him and how sweet he was with her. Becket kept careful tabs on both of them, and had a firm hand in keeping the play under control. "He doesn't know better," he reminded her when the puppy tried to eat something he shouldn't. "He's just a baby."

"Like Shane!" Tara agreed.

But the puppy was much more mobile than Shane, who was just starting to crawl, and he was quick to get into things.

They were both clearly tiring out, though, and Vivian knew that her window of opportunity for getting food into Tara was rapidly closing. She dished up plates for everyone—a tiny serving cut into little pieces for Tara, and a few noodles cooling at the side of her own for Shane—and called them in to eat.

The puppy followed them into the kitchen and sat to beg, his tail sweeping behind him.

"I don't have any puppy food," Vivian realized, putting a bowl of water down for him. "Do you think that canned meat would be okay?" She had a nearly expired can of roast beef in the back of the cabinet.

Becket shrugged, reminding Vivian what his bare shoulders had looked like. "I don't think it will hurt him."

They talked a little about pets as Vivian portioned a little of the can onto one of Tara's plastic plates and the puppy wolfed it down and came to beg at the table for more.

"I had a turtle for a while, growing up," Becket said. "It was hard to cuddle."

"My family had a cat when I was little. She

was the grouchiest, least-friendly feline that had ever called itself domestic, but she was a great mouser. She lived to be twenty-one years old and spent the last year of her life on people's laps like she'd just figured out that it was an awesome thing."

Vivian told herself that talking about laps did not mean she had to imagine herself in Becket's lap.

"This is great lasagne," Becket said sincerely.

"Frozen from the wholesale warehouse," Vivian said honestly. "It's one of those things that I love but never have the time to make from scratch, so I'm really glad it bakes so well from store bought."

She got up to get the starving puppy a second serving of canned beef, which was eaten much more slowly, the final pieces disdained altogether as he came to make the rounds of the table again, hoping for superior lasagne offerings.

"He's so cute!" Tara said, paying more attention to him than to her meal. "Look how cute he is, Mommy!"

"Eat your food," Vivian said automatically. "He *is* very cute, but we can't feed him at the table."

It wasn't long before he'd fallen over on his

side, his head a warm weight on Vivian's foot, and was snoring gently.

Tara didn't act like she would last much longer, but she ate much more of her plate than Vivian expected. Shane was looking done in by the excitement. He was starting to sway in place.

"I'd better get them down before they fall down," Vivian observed. She didn't want the cozy meal to end, really, but Becket's plate was empty, and she'd polished hers off as well, and she didn't want to hit that point past tired that kids could get to where it was impossible to settle them for bed.

"I'm not tired," Tara protested, rubbing her eyes.

"Can I help you with something?" Becket immediately offered. When he stood and pushed back his chair, the puppy woke, leapt to his feet and barked once, then staggered over to finish off his plate of food before falling asleep in the middle of it with his mouth half full.

"If you could keep Tara eating," Vivian suggested, "I'll go put Shane down."

"We can do that," Becket said, with a conspiratorial wink at Tara as he sat back down.

Becket tried not to stare after Vivian too obviously. She was so beautiful and graceful. She moved with incredible efficiency, doing about three things at any given time. Bending over to pick up Tara's dropped napkin turned into getting a spoonful of food into Shane, which turned into a bite of her own food. Somehow, she still never spoke with her mouth full.

When she left with Shane, he found himself with all of Tara's attention.

As kids sometimes did, she went shy and ducked her head.

"Do you like the lasagne?" Becket asked her.

"Uh huh," she said.

"I understand you go to day care?"

"Uh huh."

"Do you like day care?"

"Uh huh."

"I'm going to wash up some dishes," Becket said.

"Uh huh."

"Keep eating!"

"Uh huh."

Becket gathered up the empty dishes and Shane's tray insert, and made a sink of soapy water. The drainer was full, so he spent some time figuring out where the dry dishes went, soliciting Tara's help as he went.

He tried to puzzle through his unicorn's insistence that they were exactly where they ought to be and make sense of the parts of Vivian's life that he understood. She was definitely not a shifter. Tara definitely was, though Becket still had no idea what. She went to day care, although she was at an age that was risky for a shifting child to be in a social setting like that.

Shane wasn't a shifter, yet, but he was still young enough that he might grow into it.

And where was their father? Both children had distinctly Asian features, and Vivian's last name suggested they'd been married. Shane was not that old—eight months, by Becket's rather knowledgeable guess.

It was unnerving, being so attracted to Vivian, and so enamored of her family, and not knowing where he might fit in it. He shouldn't fit in it at all, probably, but instinct was telling him unmistakable that *here* and *now* was just right. He felt giddy and excited, on the brink of...he wasn't even sure what.

He found aluminum foil to cover the lasagne with and tetrused some space in the fridge for it. He could hear Shane babbling and the sound of Vivian's gentle voice reading, but couldn't quite make out any words to it. The baby gave a sleepy cry of protest, then subsided.

"Oh, you didn't have to do all of that!" Vivian said, coming back empty-handed. "I'm sorry, that all took so much longer than I expected."

"It's no trouble," Becket promised. "Thank you so much for feeding me!"

Tara had finished her food and Vivian praised her and wiped her face off.

"I'm not sleepy," Tara said preemptively.

"You might not be sleepy, but I bet you're tired, sweetheart."

Tara went to try to play with the puppy while

Vivian wiped down the table, but he was soundly asleep now, paws twitching with dreams.

"I'll talk to my neighbors tomorrow," Vivian said. "I don't think any of them have puppies, but maybe they know where he came from. He looks healthy, he must have a family."

Becket certainly wasn't going to mention the idea of a less than welcoming home in front of Tara. "I'll hang up some signs, too," he said. "There can't be that many lost golden retrievers of this age and nature in the neighborhood."

"My puppy!" Tara sang happily. She was piling stuffies around him and had even wedged a pillow under his limp head.

Becket exchanged a layered look over her head with Vivian. "I hope I haven't set up any unreasonable expectations."

Vivian shot him a look that suggested she was considering exactly what kind of expectations, reasonable or not, that he'd set and was not entirely displeased by her options.

"Tara," she said mildly. "It's time for bed."

Becket's unicorn actually capered in his head and he had to rein in his own hopeful expectations.

CHAPTER 10

Tara could be slow when she didn't want to do something. She could stretch a meal into an hour or more and getting her dressed was sometimes the battle for an entire morning. Trying to hurry her through the grocery store was like trying to push water uphill with a potato masher.

"Do you want me to brush your teeth for you, honey?"

Vivian liked the *theory* of letting Tara do things alone in order to learn the skills she would need and often fought with her own impulse to just do it herself because then it would get things done in something less than a geological era.

"I can do it," Tara insisted, polishing each

tooth with a careful thoroughness more war-
ranted for fine silver or an archeology dig.

"I think they're done, darling."

"The dennist says I have to brush each one!"
Tara protested.

Vivian was pretty sure Tara had already
brushed more teeth than she actually had, but
made herself be patient. She didn't want to think
about how bored Becket must be getting, waiting
for them to be finished.

It was so exciting and nerve-wracking,
knowing that he was just outside the door, sitting
in her living room. A real, flesh and blood man,
who genuinely seemed as interested in her as she
was in him. Vivian hadn't felt so alive in a very
long time. This wasn't just focusing on her kids
or her job or her responsibilities, this was something she wanted for herself.

It gave her a moment of pause, because there
was no way to think about *something she wanted*
without thinking about the last person who had
made her feel like this.

Jin would want her to enjoy this, Vivian realized in a bittersweet rush. The last thing in the
world that he would want was for her to be alone
forever, martyring herself for a memory. He

would be first in line pushing her to have fun, to let herself love again.

Was it too early to be thinking about love?

Vivian reminded herself that Becket was leaving in the spring and moving on to a new clinic, that even if this was a thing, it was a thing with an end date. She didn't need to be investing her whole heart into what was essentially temporary.

Finally, about seventy-two teeth, a lengthy trip to the toilet and an agonizingly long bedtime ritual later, Tara tripped out in her pajamas to say goodnight to her puppy and Dr. Becket, who was miraculously still there, and not a figment of Vivian's imagination at all. He put down his phone to smile warmly at them and Vivian reminded herself that this was definitely not love.

Yet.

"What's his name?" Tara wanted to know, bending over in that impossibly flexible way that children could to put her head upside down on the floor next to the puppy. She capered around that way, trying to coax him into waking up, and got a brief thump of his tail on the floor.

"We're not naming him," Vivian protested. "Say goodnight. The tuck-in train is leaving the station right now."

Tara gave the puppy one last pat and straightened up. She paused shyly where Becket was still sitting by the kitchen table. "Good night, Docker Becket," she said. She was carrying one of her stuffed animals, a floppy donkey name Dinky, and waved one of its legs at him.

Stronger men than Becket would have melted at that.

"Good night," he said gravely in return. "Sweet dreams."

Vivian herded her back to her room, expertly nipping every side trip in the bud. "You've already gone potty, remember? You don't need to clean that up now. We can look out the window in the morning."

There was less protest than usual, and Tara was asleep before she remembered to ask for a book. Vivian kissed her forehead and tucked the blankets up around her shoulders, then closed the door and returned to the kitchen.

Becket was coming past the table with Tara's dirty dishes just as Vivian was coming in, and she misjudged the distance they had in the space before the island.

"Oops!" Vivian was sure that she should be used to her tremendous new girth by this point, but the size of her breasts continued to surprise her, and she was constantly bumping them into things like doorframes and handsome doctors. "Sorry."

"It was my fault," he said chivalrously, though it was clearly Vivian's miscalculation that had caused the collision.

"No, it was these things," Vivian said, seeing no point in trying to pretend they didn't exist. "I feel a bit like its false advertising, I'm usually barely a B cup, but they took their duties extremely seriously, and now I feel like an unbalanced bicycle, ready to tip over at any moment and I run into *everything*."

For a moment, Becket was quiet and Vivian was afraid that he was going to be dismayed by her frankness.

Then his face split into a grin and he gave a great, honest belly laugh. He was a doctor, she should have trusted that he could talk about bodies honestly. "Are you planning to breastfeed for long?" he asked professionally.

"As long as Shane wants to, really. He eats plenty of solids now, which simplifies day care, but nursing is a nice wind-down at night still. I'd just like these girls to get the message that they don't need to make as much now. They're convinced I'm starving him to death, I think."

Becket chortled. "They'll catch up with the times, I imagine."

"Eventually," Vivian agreed with a giggle.

He finished washing and she dried and put the last dishes away. This was as nice as having the kitchen table clear; Vivian wished she always had the time and energy to do it. She was usually washing dishes as she cooked, because she needed them for that meal.

"Thanks again for dinner," Becket said. He was keeping a carefully respectful distance from her, probably knowing now exactly how ill-prepared she was to judge her own depth.

He was also making no move to *leave*. And Vivian didn't really want him to.

"Becket," she said, just exactly as he said, "Vivian…"

She chuckled and hung up the dish towel. "Guests first," she insisted.

"Crystal made it clear that you were single," he said hesitantly.

"I am not terribly surprised by that," Vivian said, feeling painfully hopeful. "She can be astonishingly meddlesome."

"But she didn't tell me anything about Shane and Tara's dad."

And that was important, Vivian recognized.

Was she in the middle of a messy divorce? Was she emotionally compromised? It was clear that she and Becket liked each other, quite a lot, and she didn't think that it was coincidence that had brought him to her door with a lost puppy.

Was it instinct? Did he have the shifter magic telling him how good they might be together? Had it led him to a lost puppy who needed a family?

The puppy in question was still sleeping on the kitchen floor. Vivian had nudged him bonelessly into a corner after nearly tripping on him several times. He hadn't so much as twitched an eyelid during his slide across the linoleum.

"Do you want a drink?" she offered.

"Just water."

"Scared I might seduce you?" Vivian teased him.

Becket gave another deep, genuine laugh. "I want to say yes clear-headed," he said, and the air between them went sizzling with the tension that had been underlying every word before.

Vivian was tempted to take a stronger drink herself, but poured them both tumblers of water out of courtesy. She almost led him to the couch, where it might be easier to climb into his lap and kiss him, but Becket took a seat at the kitchen table before she could.

Alright, this was a *conversation*. This was feeling out the ground between them. This was being sensible and adult. He deserved to know where she was coming from, so that they could make the most of this potential connection.

And honestly, Vivian was expecting a confession out of him, an admission that he was a shifter. At least, she guessed he was. Tara had called him tingly, and he had that innate grace that many shifters had. He also frequently looked as if he was arguing with himself...or a voice in his head.

She was glad that they were smart enough to be forward with each other, to put it all on the literal table between them and then make smart choices about where they went next. Even if she and her inappropriate breasts did really just want him to stop talking and bend her over that table, instead.

"It's hard to know where to start," she said honestly. "Jin and I got married five—no, almost six—years ago. He died in a car accident about a year ago." A little over a year ago, Vivian realized. It had been Labor Day weekend, and they were into October now. "I'm sure you understand how babies are made, Shane was born about five months after he died."

"You must miss him."

His face looked complicated, which Vivian was painfully familiar with. As hard as grief was, she thought that there was something even harder about trying to deal with someone who was grieving. Losing someone was straight-for-ward and full of pain and yes, it was hard wrestling with all the leftover love. But trying to comfort someone through heartbreak was fraught with not wanting to diminish their agony at the same time you wanted to help protect them from it.

She could appreciate that struggle.

"I'm not going to say that you just up and get over something like that. We loved each other a lot," Vivian's breath caught, despite her efforts to speak evenly. "It wasn't a perfect marriage, but we were a team. But I went on. I'm still…going on. Life doesn't stop when someone else dies."

She didn't want this to be a grief talk. She didn't want to spend this rare moment, when her children were both asleep, wallowing in pity. She had a gorgeous guy sitting across the table from her, and a quiet house. But Becket still wasn't speaking and she wasn't sure how to get them back to laughing over her breasts or acknowledging their attraction for each other.

Vivian took a sip of her drink, giving him space to start his own *let's be honest* moment, then nearly wore the water when he shoved his chair back forcefully and stood up.

For a moment, she thought that maybe he'd decided to skip the discussion altogether and come kiss her at last, but when she got control of her glass and looked up, his face wasn't full of the lust she hoped for or the pity she dreaded.

It was fear and regret and…anger? She didn't think it was directed at her.

"I have to go," he said, and when Vivian sat dumbly, waiting for him to explain, he turned on his heel and stormed out, grabbing his damp jacket as he left, slamming the door behind him so hard that the windows rattled.

Vivian went back over the conversation in her mind, trying to figure out where it had gone so terribly wrong, until a small, cold nose pressed against a gap above her sock.

She looked down into mournful brown puppy eyes.

"I guess it's you and me, puppy," she said. He had one of Tara's stuffies hanging from the corner of his mouth.

CHAPTER 11

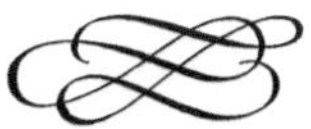

Becket welcomed the cold, driving rain on his wholly inadequate coat. It must be only a few degrees from snowing. His ears ached and his pants, still damp, felt like they were freezing onto his skin as he walked.

He fought instinct and ignored his unicorn, not trusting them to do anything but lead him straight back to Vivian's warm, welcoming house.

But he didn't belong in that bright, cozy place with that amazing woman, so he used the GPS on his phone to figure out where he was and stalk back to his rental.

He hadn't locked the door behind him when instinct drove him out, but apparently no one was out burgling in the quiet neighborhood on such an ugly night. He didn't have much to steal anyway; he'd learned to travel light, to keep from collecting things and stuff, because he'd just be moving on soon anyway.

We don't have to, his unicorn protested, with a wordless yearning for *home* and *roots*.

You know that we do, Becket snarled in return.

He didn't want to admit it, any more than his inner unicorn—now sulking—wanted to.

Vivian had just gotten over a huge grief. She'd lifted herself out of despair and the last thing Becket could do was plunge her right back into that darkness.

If she'd been divorced, or single by choice, or any of the other possibilities that Becket had clung to, maybe he could convince himself that a winter fling wasn't the worst idea in the world.

He even toyed with the idea that he could just leave her, fabricate a fight, maybe, lie about another life? Anything to give her a reason not to pursue him. She didn't *have* to know that he'd died.

Children had complicated that plan, but being widowed? Recently, tragically widowed? Becket could imagine nothing more cruel than putting her through all of that heartache again.

And then he'd seen the invitation in her eyes,

the acceptance and honesty, and he couldn't face it with anything less.

He'd caved and fled, instead of being half as truthful as she'd been. He could have told her everything, let her make of it what she would. She must know about shifters, if Tara was one, and he might have trusted that she'd be understanding of his dilemma.

But he was desperately afraid that she'd be *too* understanding, that she wouldn't stop him from breaking her heart, even if she knew that she should.

No, this was definitely the right path. Keep it distant and professional. Nurture her as nothing more than a friend and a coworker. Nip anything else in the bud. It was absolutely clear that he'd almost made a terrible mistake with her.

Whatever his unicorn insisted, whatever instinct tried to tell him, Vivian could never be the lover and partner he'd briefly imagined she might be. He refused to entangle her in another tragedy and bring her any more pain.

He was still wearing her sweatshirt, a souvenir from some kind of school in the tropics, and he pulled it off and couldn't quite keep himself from burying his face into the plush cotton. It smelled like her house—like new baby and lasagne, whatever fabric sheets she used in the dryer, and a little bit like her shampoo, damp with rain.

It smelled like home and Becket was alarmed at the depth of his longing.

It wasn't just sex that he wanted—though it was rather undeniably that, too. He wanted that home he'd been a part of for a brief meal. He wanted the dinner table chatter, and the frank banter, and the domestic chores, and the happy, noisy, companionship that his life was so painfully lacking. He even wanted—

Becket froze and took his nose from the sweatshirt.

He'd left the puppy there.

He'd completely forgotten about the sleeping canine and left him there to be Vivian's responsibility, on top of storming mysteriously out like some kind of drama queen, without a word of explanation.

He was a complete, careless clod, and he wouldn't blame Vivian for being furious with him.

How was he going to make this up to her? How could he possibly make any of this right?

Becket went to get a fresh shirt and turned on the oven.

He could start by making cookies.

CHAPTER 12

Vivian slept poorly.

Part of it was her own tangled up emotions.

She'd clearly been too frank and forward with Becket. She had too much baggage to make a relationship possible. She'd torpedoed her chance at the hot fling that Crystal was trying to lead her into and probably strained her working relationship with one of the best doctors the clinic had ever had. They'd be lucky if he didn't quit early.

She came on entirely too strong. She shouldn't have invited him to stay for dinner. She should never have talked so much about her dead husband. If she had turned him away at the door with his lost puppy, with a simple and honest,

"No, that's not ours," none of this would have happened.

Was it him? Was it her? Was she even *ready* for a new guy?

Doubt had her tossing and turning for the part of the night she was in bed.

And part of her wretched night was the puppy.

He whined from the bathroom for so long, so stridently, that Vivian feared that he would wake Tara and Shane, so she spent an uncomfortably long time sitting next to the bathtub trying to soothe him into sleep. Eventually, he seemed to settle, but Vivian found herself sleeping fitfully, listening for him to go off again as she wrestled with her restless brain.

At four in the morning, he howled until he really did wake Tara, who let him out of the bathroom to pee on the living room carpet.

"He's sowwy, Mommy!" Tara assured her as Vivian herded him out the back door with a makeshift leash and collar from one of her belts. "He didn't mean to! It was an assident!"

"I'm not mad," Vivian said. She was too tired to be mad. "But he has to learn to go outside."

The puppy didn't have anything left to do outside but sniff around and try to play with leaves, and Vivian brought him back in, not at all sure she'd taught him a single thing.

She let Tara play with him as she cleaned up the mess, trying to keep him out of the cleaning fluid as it soaked in.

They fed him more from the can of meat, and when Shane woke up, they had time to go for a walk around the block, Tara delightedly holding his makeshift leash.

The sun wouldn't be up for a little while yet, but dawn still smudged the sky. They were all dressed warmly, Shane snuggled up in a baby carrier crushing her breasts, and there was frost on all of the leaves still clinging to the trees.

It was a magical morning, and Vivian was sure that she would have missed it altogether on any other day, rushing from the house to the car to the clinic without pausing to notice the beauty of the colored sky and cold, clear taste of the air. Without the puppy to walk, she certainly wouldn't have had a chance to scuff her feet through rustling drifts of leaves, or watch Tara chase the golden dog into piles of crunchy red and orange and yellow.

She didn't trust the puppy's sense of recall yet, so she kept him on the leash, and had to untangle Tara several times as they walked, trying not to fall over with Shane's wiggly weight pulling her off-balance.

They all laughed, even Shane, with his head leaned far back so he could look up at the sky, his breath like dragon smoke from his mouth.

It was an unusually languid morning, because of their early wakeup, and Vivian found herself wishing she had someone to talk to as they walked. A grown-up.

It had been so nice, the night before.

It felt normal and right, having Becket in her house. He made her just the perfect amount of nervous and no more. She'd been eager to see where they went…and she'd blown it.

"We have to go back," she said, turning them around at a cul-de-sac.

Tara protested and the puppy pulled at his leash, but Vivian turned and herded them back.

She managed to misjudge how long it would take them to get home, and they had to hurry through all their usual morning routines with all of their usual morning rush after that. Vivian packed a hasty lunch for Tara and tried to get her to eat more than a few bites of egg and toast. "Drink your milk!" she commanded, hoping it would be enough protein to get her through.

She planned her own breakfast to be whatever

Tara didn't eat, stuffed into her mouth as they left, but came back from changing Shane to find that Tara had fed the rest to the puppy.

They looked like tragic mirrors of guilt, both of them keenly aware that they'd done the wrong thing, but were so adorable and contrite that Vivian couldn't hold it against them.

"We have to go!" she said, looking at the clock. Once again, she didn't have time to get the insurance paperwork notarized.

"Can the puppy come to Tiny Paws?" Tara wanted to know.

Vivian stared. She hadn't thought about what she was going to do with the puppy. She should have it checked for a chip, and he needed a crate. She couldn't just leave him here, and she couldn't take him to work. She knew she was already pushing the limits of tolerance at the clinic.

"No, honey, he can't go to Tiny Paws," Vivian said, though it gave her a moment of pause. It was, after all, a day care for shifters, as set up to handle animals as it was children. "He'll have to stay in the bathroom today. I'll call and make an appointment at the vet." There was no way she could leave him loose in the house. It was mostly baby-proofed, but not at all dog-proofed.

She did a quick pass of the bathroom, removing anything toxic from the counters, checking the lock on the cabinets, and taking down all the towels that would be in his reach to hang them high up over the shower curtain.

He howled miserably when Vivian shut him in, and Tara cried all the way to day care, with Shane chiming in because it sounded like fun.

Vivian considered joining them, just for solidarity.

CHAPTER 13

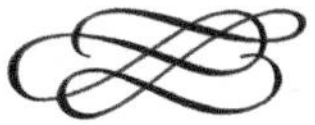

Becket brought the apology cookies to work the next day, figuring that it would only make things worse to show up with them at Vivian's house in the morning.

Vivian was already in the break room, trying to get the vending machine to take a crumpled dollar bill. "I just want beef jerky, you son of a—" The dollar ground back out and she yanked it from the feed to try the trick of smoothing it over the corner of the machine. "One goddamn package of salty, over-priced mystery animal product is not too much to ask, you snotty over-sized mechanical breadbox."

"I have cookies," Becket said from the doorway, not wanting to startle her.

The dollar tore in her hands and Vivian wadded it up and stuffed it into a pocket of her smock. "That's kind of you," she said coldly. "I didn't have time to make breakfast because we had to take our *new dog* for a walk."

The new dog that they had because of Becket. He winced. He should have insisted on taking responsibility for the puppy, but he'd been in such a hurry to escape that he hadn't thought about the magnitude of what he was leaving behind.

Vivian didn't take a cookie until Becket had put the plate down on the counter and he recognized her restraint as she all but wolfed it down.

"How is the puppy? Does he have a name yet?"

"We are not naming the dog," Vivian said around a desperate mouthful of peanut butter cookie. "We are not keeping the dog. We are finding the dog's owners and returning it. He was awake at four this morning and peed on the floor."

"Oh no," Becket said in horror.

"It was my fault," Vivian growled. "I didn't realize how badly he needed to *get out.*"

Becket winced again, sure it was a pointed reference to his abrupt departure the night before. "About last night…"

Vivian seemed to wilt against the counter.

"I'm sorry," she said, shaking her head and wiping cookie crumbs from her breasts. "I'm starving and crabby and low on sleep and sugar and you don't have to explain."

"I do," Becket said gently, but he didn't get a chance to because Crystal came sailing in at that moment.

"Oh, *cookies!*"

She slipped between them to snatch up two of the oatmeal cookies and give Vivian a sly sideways glance. "Did I hear something about *last night?*"

"Becket brought us a puppy," Vivian said dryly. "*Tara* is ecstatic."

Crystal gave a coo. "A puppy! Oh, how fun." She gave Becket a smirk and raised a cookie in salute. "I underestimated you!"

"We are not keeping the puppy," Vivian protested. "It's probably got an owner who is missing it. Oh, Crystal, I have to leave early to get it checked for a chip and make sure it hasn't eaten anything in my bathroom."

"I got you, girl!" Crystal said airily, before Becket could take the responsibility himself.

"I should do that," he protested.

"You're more critically needed here," Vivian countered. "And it's right by Tiny Paws anyway."

Tiny Paws? Her day care was named Tiny Paws? Becket wondered if it was a shifters-only, or at least shifters-friendly day care. Certainly, there seemed to be enough shifters in the area to warrant one. He hadn't expected that of Nickel City, but he was constantly running into other shifters at the grocery store and on the streets. Several of his patients were shifters, though none of their children were, yet. Bringing shifter children to non-shifter doctors was always tricky.

Crystal only then seemed to realize that there was not just *good* tension sizzling between Vivian and Becket. "I'll just take a few more of these cookies up to the front desk with me and leave you to talk about dog custody..." She took a pile, and made a show of shutting the door behind her instead of leaving it propped open the way it usually was.

"I have your shirt for you in my car," Vivian said. "I didn't want to bring it up in front of Crystal, because assumptions would be made."

"We wouldn't want that," Becket agreed.

"No, we wouldn't." Vivian's voice had an undertone to it that Becket couldn't identify. Regret? Anger? Maybe, like him, she found this whole thing hopelessly complicated.

"Vivian..."

"Crystal said there were cookies?" Doctor Jessica Jamison was a big, jovial woman that Becket already liked a lot and she came into the room with authority. "Oh, Vivian, I've got Mrs. Handel in the teal room with a boil that needs lancing. She says she won't let anyone but you handle it. I'll have Rebecca take Doctor Becket's patients while you're doing that." She scooped up a chocolate chip cookie and inspected it dubiously, like she was worried about raisins. "If you don't object, Doctor Becket?"

"Of course not," Becket had to say, because what else could he say? That he jealously wanted to keep Vivian for himself because their working relationship was all that he could ever hope for now? "Mrs. Handel's boil is in good hands."

Jessica burst out laughing. "I'll remind her how lucky she is." She took a second cookie and went out, leaving the door open behind her.

"I didn't bring your sweatshirt," Becket said apologetically. "I'll wash it and get it back to you tomorrow."

"You don't have to wash it," Vivian said. "I have to do a load of clothes every day, and I can just throw it in." She finished her cookie. "I swear, when they told me I'd wash clothes a lot as a mom, I thought it was a racket. I mean, baby clothes are like this big." She demonstrated with her hand. "How can kids generate that much laundry?"

"And now you know?" Becket guessed.

"You would not believe how many changes of clothing we can go through in a day. Even Tara, who is as fastidious as they come, manages to wear half of what she eats. I swear, sometimes I change them—and myself!—twice before we even make it out the door in the morning. If I didn't do laundry every day, we'd all be walking around completely naked."

That, of course, made Becket imagine her coming to work naked, and even as he gave an involuntary shout of laughter, he knew that it was dangerous ground...and that he and Vivian would be able to navigate it.

Somehow.

CHAPTER 14

Vivian managed to dodge Crystal's leading questions and knowing looks for the entire morning. Lancing Mrs. Handel's boil was straight-forward, and for all that the little old lady was adamant that Vivian was doing it wrong, that she wasn't dressed professionally, and she'd had to wait too long to be seen, Vivian knew that she was grateful for the treatment.

She was just a strident soul who thought she had to complain to be seen. Vivian was able to steer the conversation to Mrs. Handel's grandchildren, and they compared baby stories and talked about the parts of parenting that they loved.

"The best part of being a grandmama is that I

get to give them back, all sugared up and over-tired," Mrs. Handel cackled. "Your parents should know."

"Doctor Jessica called over your antibiotic prescription," Vivian said, instead of talking about her parents, or Jin's. It was a sore spot that her parents hadn't approved of her marriage or her children, and she'd never felt welcome in Jin's parents' lives. She hadn't even told them about Shane. She was a large enough woman that her pregnancy wasn't obvious at his funeral, and although they still sent Tara gifts, she felt that they'd always been disappointed that she was a girl, not the grandson they'd hoped for.

And all day, she thought about Becket, about how they'd been on the brink of something, and what she must have said wrong to frighten him off.

She wasn't mad about the puppy, though she thought maybe she should be.

He had been a hassle, so far, but he was one of the cutest things she'd ever seen, and she could say that as the mother to two of the cutest children in the world.

She thought he was considerably less adorable when she got home to a suspiciously quiet house.

She paused at the front door, expecting

howling from the bathroom, or at least a bark in greeting, but the puppy was silent.

Vivian dumped her purse by the front door and dashed for the bathroom door, which was still shut. He couldn't have gotten out. Tara would never forgive her.

She wrenched the door open onto a scene of utter destruction.

She had expected a mess or two to clean up. But her careful removal of the towels from his reach had neglected the shower curtain itself, which was now two feet shorter all across the bottom, torn into tiny plastic pieces and shredded all across the bathroom floor. Several of the top gussets had torn, and Vivian could only imagine him yanking and growling at the curtain.

The puppy lay in the center of his cyclone of destruction and for a heart-stopping moment, Vivian feared that he'd ingested too much of the plastic fabric and died and she was never going to forgive herself and Tara wouldn't stop crying for a month.

Then he twitched and came awake the way that Shane sometimes did, all at once with a cry of outrage. Then he was shaking himself and panting happily as he came to greet her, wagging his tail enthusiastically.

She was too relieved to be angry with him, even though she wasn't sure how she was going to shower until she got a new curtain. It wasn't like she had another one lying around somewhere.

He crawled up as far into her lap as he could get, licking and chewing on her with nothing but joy.

"You nearly stopped my heart," Vivian confessed to him, gathering him up into her arms for a quick cuddle. He whined and snuggled his fuzzy little head into her neck.

She took him out, and wondered if they weren't making some house training progress, because he immediately squatted in the grass in the back yard.

More miraculously, he swiftly returned when he was done, bounding directly back into her arms.

Vivian had not asked for a dog, and she had vehemently not wanted a dog, but she had to admit that if she was going to get one anyway, she could not have asked for one that was more eager to please and loved people. He was gentle and sweet and well-behaved, except for the appetite for shower curtains. "We're not naming you yet," she reminded herself and him.

She didn't have a crate yet, so she had to put him in the footwell of the passenger seat and hope that he stayed there, which he certainly did not. She nearly ran a red light trying not to step on him as he crowded into her own footwell, and drove the final blocks holding him in her lap as he gazed out the window and tried to lick it.

Vivian managed not to have a heart attack or cause a traffic accident, and made it to the veterinary clinic in time for her appointment.

She wasn't surprised to find that he had no chip, and the vet gave him a clean bill of health, despite his diet of shower curtain and canned beef, as well as a rabies shot. "What's his name?" he asked, preparing the tag.

"We're still looking for his owner," Vivian insisted. "We're not naming him."

The vet looked at her like she was protesting just a little too much, which probably she was.

He snapped a few photos and promised to hang signs. Vivian sighed and bought a bag of overpriced puppy chow, a collar, and a leash. She picked the pink set, because she knew that Tara would like it best.

CHAPTER 15

Becket rang the bell at Vivian's house and tried not to fidget. She deserved the whole truth, every part of it, and he had no idea how he was going to tell it to her.

He should have brought cookies.

Maybe cookies with his confession written out in raisins.

That would probably take a lot of cookies.

"We're not accepting any more pets," Vivian said, when she opened the door. She stood aside and invited him in anyway, leading him back into the kitchen where Shane was unsuccessfully experimenting with a sideways spoon and a bowl of green baby food.

"I don't have any more pets to foist off on you," Becket promised. "I actually came to get the puppy until you—until *I*—find its owner. It's not fair that you'd have to take care of my charity case."

The words were the worst mistake that he could have made—much worse than neglecting to bring cookies—and he caught Vivian's look of warning and his unicorn's twang of instinct moments too late.

Tara was standing just inside the kitchen, trying to coax the puppy to drink from a bowl, and she looked up in horror. "He's my puppy!" she insisted. "You can't have him!"

"Tara," Vivian said gently. "You know we're only taking care of him until we find his family. They're probably missing him."

Tara snapped.

Becket wasn't sure if it was his words that did all the damage, or if she was tired, or hungry, or if her socks were too tight, but he watched her face get very red and had enough experience with children to know exactly what was coming next.

"My puppy!" she screamed, throwing herself bodily over the bewildered dog. "My puppy!"

She said more, but between her screaming

and crying and Vivian trying to protect her from the puppy, who thought it was all a delightful game and was joining in with yips and growls and carelessly snapping teeth, Becket couldn't make out another single word.

Vivian picked her daughter up out of the puppy's enthusiastic reach and Tara fought her with all of her four-year-old strength, arching her back and screaming like a train whistle as she kicked and beat at Vivian in an absolutely classic meltdown.

To Becket's awe, Vivian didn't once lose her cool. She took every one of Tara's tiny blows without flinching, hugging her, but not trying to stop her or restrain her more than absolutely necessary to keep from dropping her.

"Big feelings, little girl," she murmured, as Tara cried and struggled. "Big feelings, I know."

Becket might not understand a word of Tara's strident tirade, but the emotions were clear. She felt betrayed and bereft, sure that her puppy—her best and only friend—was being ripped unfairly away forever. She was outraged by the injustice and utterly heartbroken, all of her feelings magnified by her tender age.

She sobbed and screamed and fought with Vivian, who only held her hard enough that she couldn't do any lasting harm and murmured patiently through the shrieking fit until Tara's cries had faded to muffled whimpers against Vivian's shoulder. It took a painfully indeterminate amount of time and the puppy whined and wiggled in distress and excitement through the entire thing, pressing against Vivian's calves like he was trying to soak the heartache from them with sheer willpower.

Vivian didn't apologize for the outbreak, though she exchanged one chagrined look over Tara at Becket, who felt that he could do the most good by helping Shane manage his misunderstood spoon and cleaning up the water that had splashed on the floor from the dog's dish.

"Puppy," Tara sobbed, reaching down for him and trying to squirm from Vivian's gentle arms. "My puppy." She was exhausted, and when she gave up and went limp at last, Vivian let her down onto the floor.

"Say goodnight."

Tara slowly hugged the nameless pup, cuddling into his soft ears and wrapping her chubby arms around him.

The puppy was gentle, more subdued than before her fit, and wagged his tail and licked her until Tara giggled.

"Let's go get ready for bed," Vivian said, but when she offered a hand to Tara, Tara reached both arms up to be carried.

Vivian lifted her up and took her first to the bathroom and then down the back hall.

Shane craned around to watch her go, threatening to fuss, and Becket teased him with a heaping spoonful of the baby food, which managed to miss his mouth altogether when he went to get it in.

"How much did you get into him?" Vivian asked, when she came back.

"Probably less than I got onto him," Becket said honestly. "There was a bit of a struggle. How's Tara?"

"She fell asleep," Vivian said, going to the sink. She came back with a wet washcloth and wiped down a squirming Shane, starting with his face and then each hand, and returning to the face because he'd managed to smear more onto it.

"Baba!" he protested, flailing his arms. "Bah!"

"I want to tell you some things," Becket said, as she lifted Shane up out of the high chair and managed to clean off the high chair with one free hand. "Some things that aren't easy to say. I don't…want to make your life harder than it is."

"You don't get to decide what makes my life harder," Vivian said with an absolutely staggering amount of serenity. "Tell me your piece and I'll make my own choices from there."

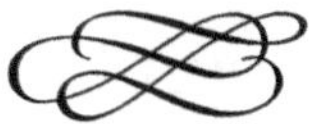

Vivian wasn't exactly sure why Becket was looking at her like she was something remarkable. She was an ordinary human woman trying to make her way through a dizzying secret world of magic and protect her children, more exhausted than admirable. It broke her heart into pieces to hear Tara cry and to know that her little girl felt betrayed and didn't have the capacity to understand the larger world and all its beauty and cruelty yet.

All she could do was hold onto her core of certainty that this was a moment that would wash over her and be gone. All she had to do was weather the wave of it the best she could.

"I'm a shifter," Becket said.

"I'd guessed as much," Vivian said.

"I'm not a normal shifter, though."

"I'd guessed that, too."

"I'm a unicorn."

"That makes sense."

He looked disappointed, like he was expecting more surprise from her. Probably, he was. Even people who knew about shifters usually only knew about the ordinary animal shifters. Unicorns and dragons and elementals were shrouded in even more secrecy, like layers of an onion.

Vivian only nodded, then dropped her own bomb. "So was Jin."

"Oh." Becket stared at her. "Oh! And Tara?"

Vivian was still nodding, because she was exhausted and had forgotten to stop. "A Chinese unicorn. A kirin."

"Tara said she was *lucky*."

"I didn't know much about kirin," Vivian said. "Jin didn't tell me about them until Tara was born and even then, I don't think he told me everything. I think he thought he was protecting me." She didn't mean her tone to be quite as full of warning as it came out, but Becket looked tellingly guilty.

"I don't...want to keep anything from you," he

said so reluctantly that Vivian knew that he actually did.

"Spit it out, doctor," she said. "How long do I have to live?"

She'd meant it as a joke, drawn on their shared medical background, but it fell painfully, ironically flat.

"I couldn't tell you your life expectancy," Becket said grimly, "but I know mine."

Vivian blinked at him. "You know when you're going to die?" If he'd wanted surprise from her, he had it now.

"It's not perfectly exact," Becket explained. "As a unicorn, I have the ability to heal people. Magically. Glowy horn and all. Cure cancer, mend broken bones, seal up wounds. But it has a price, and every time I use it, I watch the end of my life come closer."

Vivian felt a dozen little mysteries and suspicions in her life settle into place, like ice cubes in a glass that finally slid down to make space and she closed her eyes at the shock of it. She was glad to be holding Shane, because it gave her a thing to do, to soothe and rock him while she tried to make sense of her new world order.

Jin hadn't been able to magically heal, though he, like Tara, claimed he was *lucky*. Vivian had always ascribed it to part of his sunny optimism, that what looked like luck was just a positive spin on standard circumstance. But what if it wasn't? What if he'd been able to see ahead in time, see things before they happened so that he could make good choices?

It hadn't saved his life.

And that brought her here.

"You're going to die." Vivian didn't let her gaze waver and she saw Becket struggle to hold it.

"I'm going to die."

"And you know when."

"Yes."

She absorbed that in silence for a moment. Shane was falling asleep, but not there yet, and she rocked him a little in place automatically when he started to fuss in defiance of his inevitable unconsciousness. "When?" she finally asked.

Becket gave a sigh like wind through autumn trees. "Right now? It happens in a year. If I'm careful."

"If you don't heal too many people."

Vivian thought about what it must be like to face such a decision, to know that your sacrifice was more than just an empty probability. He knew exactly what every moment of magic cost him, on a deep, personal level.

"I'm sorry," Becket said, and he sounded genuinely sorry. "It's a terrible burden and I...didn't want to put it on you. Not after what you've already been through. But I thought you should know the truth. Why we can't be together. It's not that I don't want to be."

"*Why* can't we be together, exactly?" Vivian asked.

"I can't do that to you. I can't do that to Shane and Tara. Vivian, I want to be here with you. You're gorgeous and sexy and I'm desperate to see how good we could be together. But you deserve forever and I can't give you that. I couldn't bear to hurt you and the only way not to is to try not to let anything *happen* between us."

Shane was really asleep now, completely boneless and still in her arms. Vivian's shoulder was starting to ache. She was used to his weight, but she'd already spent a long time holding Tara, who was heavier than she looked.

"I appreciate you telling me," Vivian said carefully. "I'm going to put Shane down."

She stepped over the sleeping puppy, who didn't even stir, and went to tuck the slumbering boy into his crib. He fussed sleepily for a moment but settled before she had even left the room, shutting the door quietly.

She half-expected Becket to be gone when she got back, and she had a visceral reaction to the sight of him, sitting on her couch, leaning forward to pet the puppy, who had sleepily rolled to his back for tummy rubs. It was late, but the curtains were still open and the light from the street lamps cast a curious golden light into the room.

She waited in the door to the living room for a long moment, thinking over his remarkable confession.

He knew the moment of his own death. And it wasn't that far off, in the scope of things.

Vivian didn't feel as surprised as she thought she ought to, and she examined her own reaction clinically. It made a certain amount of sense, really, falling into place with all the other bits of data that she had.

He looked up and noticed her. "I can take him home with me," he offered reluctantly. Was he reluctant to take the puppy, or to go home?

"Let him sleep," Vivian said. The puppy's paws had crossed over his chest and he looked adorably anthropomorphic sleeping on his back with his ears splayed out on the floor beneath him.

She went into the kitchen and found a bottle of wine in the back of a cabinet. It was old and she had no idea how long it had been open, but she didn't have anything stronger or fresher in the house. There were wine glasses pushed to the back of the cabinet behind the plastic tumblers, and she wiped the dust out of two of them and brought them to Becket.

"I'm pretty sure that Jin could see the future, too," she said, sitting on the couch next to him. "He sometimes did mysterious things that only made sense afterwards. He bought a big life insurance policy just a few weeks before he died."

"I don't know much about Chinese unicorns," Becket said, gravely accepting the glass. "Tara tells me she's lucky."

Vivian gave a hiccup of laughter as she poured their wine. "The day before we met she told Shane that she would be getting a yellow puppy with floppy ears."

Becket looked thoughtfully down at the unnamed retriever. "She told me about him too. It's an apt description."

"And a little too much for coincidence," Vivian said.

"Foresight *would* look a lot like luck," Becket agreed.

"Because having a shapeshifting child was not complicated enough," Vivian said dryly. She hadn't had much to drink yet, but maybe the smell of it was psychosomatic, because she impulsively volunteered, "The insurance company thinks it was a little too much for coincidence, too."

"They're refusing to pay?"

Vivian considered herself a self-sufficient and independent woman, but she could not deny the reaction that Becket's tone of voice dredged out of her. He was outraged for her, fierce and ready to fight, and Vivian had not realized how amazing it would feel to have someone who wanted to protect her after this long forced to face her battles alone. At first, her friends had been eager to help her, but as she insisted she was fine, they slowly believed her, and she was afraid that admitting any weakness would mean losing all the ground she'd gained.

"They are 'still investigating,'" Vivian said. "They say it's automatic in their system when a claim is made so soon after a policy is started, but it's been a year now, and I've had to appeal it twice for technicalities, so I'm starting to think they're going to deny it altogether."

"Are you a suspect in his death?"

"It was a drunk driving accident miles from here," Vivian said, shaking her head. "Very cut and dry."

"They shouldn't be dragging their feet," Becket said fiercely. "Aren't you furious?"

"I was really angry," Vivian said honestly. "But I was more angry with my husband. I thought that if Jin knew that he was going to die, he could have stopped it, found a loophole, changed the future, and stayed here for Tara, if not for me."

"You miss him." Becket stared into his wineglass and Vivian could hear the wistfulness in his voice.

Vivian recognized the minefield that they were traveling. This was the conversation that had driven him to flee last time. They were close together on the couch—it had an aged sag to it that eventually sent anyone sitting on it to the center. His thigh was not quite touching hers, close enough that she could feel the warmth of him.

She swirled a taste of the wine in her mouth. She didn't want to drink so much that her decisions were compromised, but at the same time, she didn't particularly want to face this conversation sober.

"I grieved for a long while," she said frankly.

"And I did the hard work to get over it, because I chose to be here for my kids instead of living in the misery of memory. I took medication to get through the worst of it, and I did plenty of therapy. I still do. I'm not going to say that it didn't tear me up, or deny that I loved him. But I'm in a healthy space, living now and making choices for my future, whether *I* can see it or not."

"I admire that about you," Becket said quietly. "Not many people would be strong enough to do that."

"I don't know how much it's about strength," Vivian said. "It's more about common sense. I mean, I could have continued draping myself over furniture feeling sorry for myself, but it's just not that practical for paying bills and raising children."

Becket laughed and warmed by the wine, Vivian let herself sag into him. He put an arm around her.

"Did Jin tell you about instinct?"

"I know about it in theory," Vivian said. "A sense of warning. But it sounds like his sense was a little more than what most shifters have."

"Not just warning," Becket said. "It can tell us when something is right, just as much as when something is wrong. Sometimes, it's hard to make sense of it."

Vivian tried to analyze the tone in his voice. Was he trying to hint at something? *Like me?* she wanted to ask, but she didn't quite have the courage. That was a forever kind of question, and they clearly didn't have forever.

But they did have now.

"I don't need instinct to tell me that this is a good time for you to make a move," Vivian said, leaning forward to put her glass on the coffee table. "Both of my children and my new rescue are all asleep at the same time. I'm here, with you, now, and I've had just enough wine to let myself do exactly what I want to, without compromising any of my values."

"Will you regret it in the morning?" Becket asked carefully.

"You're the one who sees the future," Vivian reminded him. "Now put down that wineglass and kiss me."

CHAPTER 17

Becket didn't need a second invitation. He barely got the wineglass down on the coffee table before he was pulling Vivian into his arms.

She kissed like she lived, like she knew where she was going but she wasn't in a hurry to get there. She was warm and alive and now, all of her, entirely. They kissed and Becket ran his fingers into her hair the way he'd been dying to, touching the lines of her neck and the angle of her jaw.

They didn't spend long there, breaking to move their exploration lower and braver with each other. Mindful of her chagrin over her breasts, Becket didn't linger there, finding other places that made her hiss and shiver.

"Wait," she said near his ear. "I *guarantee* my bed is more comfortable than my couch."

Becket drew back and took a moment to gaze into her eyes. Making out in the living room was one thing, a natural progression from sitting comfortably together making major confessions, but moving to the bedroom felt like a declaration of intent. They both knew what happened next, and they were both ready to accept it.

"Lead the way," he invited.

She did, but when they got to the bedroom, untidy and lived-in like the rest of the house, and she closed the door behind them, instinct gave a sudden sizzle of warning.

"What is it?" he asked, catching Vivian's hands as she started to unbutton his shirt. "There's something bothering you."

She looked thoughtfully into his eyes. "I wasn't going to let it *stop* me," she said, not denying it.

"Tell me anyway," Becket invited.

Vivian gestured down at herself. "I have a certain amount of body dysphoria," she said frankly. "It doesn't always feel like it's my own anymore."

"Having children is bound to change you," Becket said.

"It's nothing," Vivian said, reaching for his buttons again. "I can do this."

"Wait. I want you to meet someone," Becket said, intercepting her hands again.

Vivian paused. "Are you going to show me your unicorn?" she asked with interest.

"No." Becket's unicorn was eager to be admired, but that wasn't where Becket was going. "Or at least, not now. I want to show you *you*."

Vivian wrinkled her forehead. "Me?"

Becket touched her eyebrows. "You. Your occipitofrontalis," he told her, stroking up to her hairline. "For wrinkling your brow."

She smiled and he touched her temples. "Temporalis," he said.

"I haven't had to remember these terms since I was studying for finals," Vivian said, giggling.

Becket could feel instinct gentling as Vivian relaxed. "Masseter," he said, tracing down her jaw. "Sternocleidomastoid. For eating, and smiling... and kissing." He demonstrated.

"You do know how to talk dirty," Vivian said, laughing. "I remember trapezius, and pectoralis major..." She got Becket's shirt slipped off his shoulders. "Deltoideus, biceps bracchi..." She touched them each in turn, tracing the muscles of his arms.

Becket pulled her shirt up over her head and could not quite keep himself from hissing in pleasure at the sight of her, uncovered.

"An embarrassment of riches," she said, chagrined again, but Becket took her breasts reverently in each hand.

"They are nothing to be embarrassed about," he assured her. "Your beautiful body made your children and serves them well, but that too is only part of the sum of you, in all of its shapes and sizes. You are a miracle of a machine, an absolute masterpiece. I want you to see you as I do. It might not have been you once, and maybe it won't be again, but it is right now."

He glanced up and caught a sight of their reflection in the mirror at the back of Vivian's door. "Here," he said, drawing her in front of it. "Look how gorgeous you are!"

CHAPTER 18

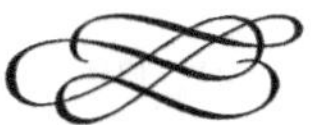

There was a mirror on the back of Vivian's bedroom door; she rarely saw it because it was almost never closed. She wanted to be able to hear Shane or Tara call for her, and she frankly didn't like what she saw in it.

She tried to look at her reflection dispassionately, and saw a harried version of herself with oversized breasts on a padded frame. She'd been athletic once, but pregnancy had softened her. She was still strong, but less fit, and her hair, which had been thick and full in pregnancy, was distressingly limp and lackluster.

It was easier to look at Becket than at herself, comparing her memory with her reality.

He was so effortlessly handsome, and almost

impossibly well-built, with muscles everywhere they ought to be, and strong limbs. Long fingers lifted her hair so he could kiss her neck.

"You're beautiful," he said firmly. He found a line along her cheekbone down her neck. "Painters through the ages have tried to capture curves like yours. Your skin is intoxicating. Your legs, your hips…" he touched all of her and Vivian couldn't deny her reaction or his sincerity.

She looked back at herself as he drew his hands over every part and saw her reflection through his eyes. Her hair might be less full than it was once, but it still had a pleasing softness and subtle curl. Her waist was less trim, but her hips were sexy and curvy now in a way they hadn't been before. Her skin was flushed with healthy desire. Some people liked freckles.

His cock was pressing against her back, and Vivian was quite sure that his reaction was in no way forced.

"Your most beautiful part is here," he said, drawing a finger over her forehead.

"My occipitofrontalis?" Vivian said breathlessly. She wiggled her eyebrows.

"Your brain," Becket said, turning her away from the mirror to face him. "The lump of electrical energy that makes you as smart and loving and funny and indomitable as you are. Every time you say or do something, I fall further in love with you."

"Love?" Vivian said in astonishment. She paused to examine her own reaction to the idea. It was alarming, to think of loving someone after so little time, but if there was anyone she could…

"It could be, don't you think?" Becket was clearly in for a penny, in for a pound, and Vivian decided that she liked that about him. He hadn't offered to sleep with her until they'd talked about where they might go with things, making sure she knew all the stakes and telling her all of his secrets.

He *was* a unicorn, Vivian thought, regardless of his shifter form.

He was thoughtful and kind and competent, big-hearted and light-humored. He was honest, which could not have been easy.

And he wanted her, the way she wanted him, in ways that were both complicated…and not.

"It could be love," Vivian agreed. "It really could."

And this part of it was easy, quietly uncovering each other the rest of the way, naming the muscle groups and demonstrating their uses as they went.

"My favorite muscle," he said with a hiss, when she drew her nails tentatively down his shaft.

"Not technically a muscle," Vivian teased him, slipping her fingers around him.

"Are we being technical?" Becket asked, his voice catching as she stroked to his tip.

"We're using Latin names," Vivian pointed out. "That seems pretty technical."

They laughed together, though the joke was weak, because they were both full of joy and desire. Vivian might have explained it away with endorphins, released by the anticipation of their act, or dopamine, but she didn't care for the reasons now, only the pleasure.

CHAPTER 19

$\mathcal{B}$ecket was courteous with Vivian's breasts. He teased them gently. She was strong under her softness, and clear about her boundaries, leading him to touches and caresses that did the most for her while she explored his own body.

"I don't have a condom," she said sensibly, when one thing was *definitely* going to lead to another. "I love my children, but I'm not interested in another right now."

Becket actually had to swallow back the idea of having a baby with Vivian. He didn't have the luxury to think about that option. "I've had a vasectomy," he said. "I didn't want to leave a child behind that I couldn't promise to be a dad to."

"You really are a unicorn," Vivian said in awe.

When she took him to the bed, they fit together perfectly and it took all of Becket's self-control not to simply lose himself in the feeling of sliding into her hot, wet lips and having her body wrapped around him.

They moved together cautiously at first, but swiftly found a desperate, pounding rhythm that had her crying softly and clutching at his shoulder. "More!" she begged. "Yes!"

Becket obliged, thrusting harder and faster until she was gasping in release and going limp and then he slowed, clinging to his own crest of need until she'd come again in a second peak of bliss.

Then, finally, he lost himself, and he made a helpless noise when he spilled into her, blazing as hot and as hard as he'd ever felt.

They moved together for some time afterwards, slower and satisfied, riding the shared moment. He kissed her and held her close, reveling in the skin between them, and the pounding of their pulses.

There was a bathroom off of Vivian's bedroom, and they showered together with the same careful attention to each other that they'd made love. The puppy had chewed off the lower half of the shower curtain, but Becket was able to move the curtain rod down so that the mangled curtain was mostly inside the tub enclosure. Water splashed over the top, but it was less of a mess than it would have been up higher.

"Becket," she said, and he loved how she said his name. "Will you stay tonight?"

He loved that even more.

Most of all, he was glad he didn't have to figure out how to ask. "I would like that a *lot*," he said.

Becket dressed and went to take the puppy outside as Vivian towel-dried her hair.

The puppy did not particularly want to go out, trying several times to fall bonelessly over as Becket herded him to the door.

Becket finally picked him up and deposited him into the unruly grass of the back yard. That earned him a mournful and betrayed look from the puppy, followed by a tired, sniffing wander that resulted in a token amount of pee along the fence.

The puppy was eager to return to the house, and the expedition seemed to belatedly energize him. He bounded into the bedroom and bounced to put his paws on the side of the bed. He hopped a few times, whining and straining. After he'd fallen back down several times as Becket un-dressed, he took pity on the dog and lifted him up.

Vivian, returning from checking on the kids, hung her bathrobe on a hook by the door and went to her dresser. "The puppy should not be in bed," she said severely. "I'll have to get a crate for him tomorrow. I should shut him in the bath-room for the night. I can put some old towels in the bathtub."

"But, he's so cute," Becket protested, trying not to be too obvious in his enjoyment of Vivian's naked show. "Look how sleepy he is."

Hellbent on making a liar out of him, the puppy wrestled and chewed on the blankets and tried to burrow under them, his little tail thumping on the mattress.

"If he pees on the bed, you're cleaning it up."

"Yes, ma'am," Becket agreed. He could resist her no longer, and left the puppy stalking a pillow to come and take the pajamas she was pulling from a drawer away from her so that he could hug her with the whole naked length of himself.

It wasn't a sexy hug, exactly, but it was far from unsexy, full of comfort and connection.

He drank in the feeling of her all along him, relishing the warmth of her skin and the fall of her damp hair. She gave a little sigh and relaxed into him, fitting against him like they'd been made for each other. Even though he was thoroughly satisfied, she made him feel completely content and somehow more alive than he'd been in a long time.

This mattered.

It wasn't just sex, it was touch and trust. It was the surrender of the distance he'd been trying so hard to keep from everyone. But Vivian wasn't just anyone, she was his happiness. It was almost like she was the embodiment of all the joy he'd denied himself in his relentless pursuit of making what was left of his life have meaning.

It was like suddenly having roots, but the idea didn't terrify him the way it always had, even with the bittersweet knowledge that their time was finite.

CHAPTER 20

Vivian woke in a cold panic and listened, sure that there was some emergency she needed to leap up and solve but completely unable to figure out what it might be. She couldn't remember the last time she'd slept so deeply and she was disoriented and confused by the faint morning light through the curtains. Shane usually got her up much earlier than this. And there was a puppy that still had no name that would need a walk. Tara had gone to sleep crying, was she awake and upset?

She could hear Shane now, but to her surprise, he wasn't crying for her, he was babbling and banging...on his high chair?

It was strange to find herself naked—usually

she wore a sleeping bra at the least, because her breasts were otherwise inconvenient even just for turning over. It was like sleeping with restless hippos attached to her chest. But they had not disturbed her deep sleep in the slightest, even though they were achingly full now.

She dressed swiftly and opened the bedroom door.

The puppy noticed her first, and gave a yelp of greeting. He came at a comical staggering gallop to whine and wiggle adoringly at her feet, jumping to put his paws on her legs.

"No jumping," Vivian scolded. It was adorable while he was a puppy the size of a loaf of bread, but she knew that it was a terrible habit to encourage. She crouched to greet him and he licked and chewed on her fingers and threw himself onto his side for belly rubs.

"Do you need to go out?" she asked him, charmed by his cuteness and still not sure what time it was or which way was up.

"I just took him out," Becket called from the kitchen and Vivian went in, nearly tripping over the puppy as he skipped back up to his feet just as she stepped over him.

Shane was sitting in his high chair, the floor around him speckled in soft peas that the puppy immediately went to vacuum up. Shane gave a cry of joy at the sight of Vivian and stretched his arms out demandingly.

"The peas have been disdained," Becket told her cheerfully. "I didn't want to wake you up, but I do think that Shane would prefer what you have to offer."

Vivian unbuckled him from his chair and he signed milk and immediately started tugging on her shirt. "I think he would," she agreed with a laugh. "I can take him to the bedroom…"

"Wherever you like," Becket said breezily. "But there are pancakes on the griddle and if you stay, I can feed you while you feed him."

The promise of food made Vivian's stomach rumble. She could not remember the last time she'd had the time to make a full breakfast before work.

And a full breakfast it was, with little breakfast sausages—fried crispy, not just microwaved —and a glass of orange juice. Vivian fed herself, but she let Becket cut up the food and smother it in syrup so she could eat one handed while Shane nursed with her on the couch.

He even got Tara up and dressed and set her at her own breakfast. "She doesn't like a lot of syrup," Vivian warned him. "Don't give her too much sausage."

But the promise of playing with the puppy when she was done was like magic and Tara wolfed down her breakfast with speed that Vivian was not sure she had ever witnessed. The last piece of sausage was fed to the eager retriever puppy despite Vivian's protests about encouraging begging and they were playing gently together on the floor when she took Shane to change him and get dressed for day care.

She exchanged a casual kiss with Becket when she returned, as natural as breathing, and to her astonishment, Tara was already ready to go, holding a bag bulging with lunch that she would never be able to eat.

"I already cleared bringing the puppy into the clinic with Crystal," Becket told him. "I'll stop at the pet store on the way in and get a crate, as well as some food and dishes."

Tara looked up at him in sudden reservation. "He's my puppy!" she insisted. "His name is Dandelion."

"We're not naming the puppy," Vivian said, though she hesitated to ruin the beautiful morning they were having. She didn't want to set off another temper tantrum, but she couldn't string Tara along, either. "We can't keep him, honey. We have to find his owners and take him to his home. They probably miss him."

"But *I'll* miss him!" Tara said with her firm four-year-old grasp of logic. Her eyes were very big and her chin was quivering.

"I can bring him with me to visit every day until we find his owners," Becket promised, looking hopefully over Tara's head at Vivian.

She couldn't help but think about what those visits would be like, how nice it was to have Becket around, to have a reason to clean her house…and wear matching underclothes.

CHAPTER 21

Becket floated through his day on the memory of Vivian in his arms, of Vivian's bare skin, of her blue eyes when she told him to take her to the bedroom. Her kisses. Her surrender…

He swallowed hard and reminded himself that they were at work and he was trying to remain professional.

The puppy was a hit at the clinic. After some Internet research, Crystal theorized that the puppy was part of a litter that had been found abandoned by animal control. He went through at least seven names.

"We're not naming him," Vivian insisted, when

they were pausing at a lull in appointments in the front office at the same time.

"You *have* to!" Crystal insisted. "Look at those darling eyes! And those darling ears! And those darling *paws*! What about Killer?"

The puppy, looking very darling indeed, was gnawing ferociously on a bone nearly as big as he was, growling and shaking his head.

"I am not naming him," Vivian protested. "And if I was, I would not name my four-year-old's dog *Killer*."

"That's totally inappropriate," Becket agreed. "He needs a name like Eugene or Winchester."

"Stop naming the dog, Becket!"

Vivian's voice was filled with laughter and Becket might have believed that he was only imagining the warmth in it, but Crystal gave them a very suspicious look as she left.

When Vivian closed the break room door, he had a moment of ridiculous hope. Surely she didn't plan to have sex with him here, now? His own body was certainly willing, his cock coming to attention at the very suggestion of it.

But Vivian had considerably more self control than he did, and after she kissed him and gave him a promising stroke through his pants, she drew back. "I'd like it very much if you could talk to Tara about being a unicorn. Well, about being a shifter."

"Does she need help shifting?"

"Oh, no. Addison, at Tiny Paws, says that she's one of the best shifters there. She never changes without meaning to, and she always brings her clothing with her. But I'm worried that she doesn't know what it's like to be a unicorn."

"I'm not the same kind of unicorn," Becket reminded her. He told himself not to get distracted by the way that Vivian's breasts strained under her smock, or think too much about what they'd been like in his hands.

"I know," Vivian said with a wince. "I feel like I've done wrong by her, because I don't really have a lot of information about kirin besides what I've read in books. Maybe you could talk to her, find out what she can actually do. As much as that is possible with a four-year-old."

"I would love to," Becket said sincerely, and it wasn't hard to put aside his incredible lust to realize that he wanted to do exactly that. Tara needed a guide in the sticky world of shifters, and he truly wanted to be that guide.

Vivian's look of gratitude was a near second to the look of bliss he'd given her the night before. "Thank you. I think it's different hearing things from someone who isn't your mother, and she seems to like you. Maybe you can get her to show you the draft of the book that Addison made for her. It's a picture book called the *Kirin Who Could,* and I've read it to her probably a million times already."

"I'd love an excuse to come over after work tonight."

"You don't really need an excuse," Vivian told him, and all the lust came roaring back at her suggestive tone. How was it only mid-morning? How was he going to make it through a day of patching up skinned knees and diagnosing ear infections like this?

"Let me get Killer to Crystal's desk so I can get back to patients," he said reluctantly. He dared to give her one chaste kiss on the cheek before commotion in the hall had him backing politely away.

"We're not naming him Killer!" Vivian said, her eyes full of laughter.

Somehow, Becket made it through the day without dragging Vivian into the break room and locking the door to make love to her on the floor. Passing in the narrow back halls was more fun than ever, and he was quite sure that when she brushed him with her breasts it was not *all* accidental.

Crystal definitely knew that something was up, and she reiterated the coworker dating policy a few times, very innocently, and gave him knowing looks when she caught him gazing after Vivian.

Becket went home when the clinic closed, because it felt presumptuous to go directly from work to Vivian's house, and because he wasn't sure how long it would take her to collect her kids from Tiny Paws, or if she had running around to do afterwards. Should he text before showing up? Change clothes? Dress up? Comb his hair?

You're being ridiculous, his unicorn scoffed. *We should just be together. Nothing else matters.*

He got the puppy out of his crate, but the puppy sniffed around the rental house and then cried pitifully, uninterested in either food, water, or a walk.

"Yeah, this place isn't that much fun," Becket agreed.

He decided he had waited long enough already, put the leash on the puppy, and went to walk the few blocks to Vivian's house, trying not to fidget when the puppy wanted to stop and smell every tree and fence post.

"My puppy!" Tara said, flinging open the door

as Becket came up the front walk. Had she known they were coming or had she been watching for them? Nothing she did or said was strictly impossible for her to know. Even her daydreams about the puppy *could* be circumstantial.

Becket remembered his promise to Vivian to talk to Tara about shifting, but was immediately swept up in preparation for dinner, and then eating dinner, and then helping to clean up.

"I can finish these dishes and do Shane's bath," Vivian said. "Maybe you could take the puppy out back with Tara for a while."

Becket kissed her nose. "A lovely suggestion."

Tara was all-in for anything involving her puppy, and the two of them scampered out into the darkening yard with Becket following more sedately.

He let them romp for a while, chasing sticks and running in big circles, then called them back and gave each of them the end of a tug toy.

"You're a shifter," Becket said, when their play had calmed a little. "Did you know that I am, too?"

Tara looked at him with those entirely-too-wise eyes. "Yes." She said it cautiously, which made sense. It was drilled into shifter children that they couldn't talk to about their abilities with strangers, that only family was safe. "You're tingly."

"Can you guess what I am?"

Tara's face bloomed into a smile at the idea of a game. "A gopher? A hummingbird?"

"Bigger than a hummingbird or a gopher," Becket said, shaking his head.

"A cow? A deer?" She guessed a few more normal animals and he gave her more hints. "I have four legs, no wings."

"A bear? A gopher?"

When she started to loop back around to her first guesses, Becket told her, "There's another one in this yard."

Tara's eyes lit up. "A puppy! You're a puppy! Jennifer is a puppy too!"

"Not a puppy," Becket said.

Tara's face crinkled in confusion, looking around in the yard. "A bug?"

"Bigger than a gopher," Becket reminded her.

Tara's eyes got very big as she realized what he meant and she let go of the puppy's tug so abruptly that he fell backwards into a surprised sit. "A unicorn," she whispered. "Are you a kirin like me?"

The puppy realized that he had the rope toy to himself and frolicked in several circles, shaking his head until his ears flapped against his skull as he growled and worried at the tug.

"I'm not a kirin," Becket clarified. "But I *am* a unicorn."

Tara's mouth went into a little cartoon O. She would be an amazing meme, Becket thought, with the absolutely perfect expression of awe on her face.

The puppy, finding that the rope was not as much fun without someone pulling on the other end of it, trotted up and tried to tease Tara into playing again.

She ignored him, to beg Becket, "Will you show me? Will you show me? Will you show me?"

Becket made a show of looking around. "Is it safe?"

Tara did a sweep of the yard. "Our fence is tall," she said. "No one else is here. It's safe. Pwease!"

Becket had melted for less, and it wasn't often that he got a chance to show his unicorn form off, especially to an audience as appreciative as this. "I think it's safe, too," he decided, though he walked a quick circuit of the small backyard, the puppy so close on his heels that he was nearly stepped on more than once.

It wasn't a fancy yard, not that Becket had really expected intricate landscaping. There was a fallow vegetable garden in the back that his unicorn suggested might have wild onions and volunteer herbs, and it was otherwise scruffy autumn-dead lawn with several bald patches around a few mid-sized trees.

Between two of these trees, Becket came to a stop, pausing to gaze around one final time. Tara waited on the patio, twisting her hands in her skirt as she bounced in anticipation. The sun was just setting, the sky overhead darkening, but Becket knew that the girl would have no trouble seeing him as he bowed his head.

Then, in the space of a breath, he was on four legs, tossing a heavy head and feeling the whisper of his mane as it fell over his withers. For a moment, all he could do was caper, bright in the dim twilight.

Too long, his unicorn sighed happily. It had been too long since they'd had a chance to do this. He'd tried to find a place to rent with a high-fenced yard, but they were hard to find at a price he was willing to pay and proximity to the clinic had won out in the end.

The puppy, after alarm-barking at Becket's transformation, proceeded to play fearlessly at his feet, forcing Becket to step carefully towards the patio where Tara was still standing like a stone.

Was she afraid?

She should not fear us, his unicorn said, but it was with a touch of uncertainty.

Rather than risk frightening her, Becket shifted back and closed the final distance on two feet.

"You're a *real* unicorn," Tara said.

"You're a real unicorn, too," Becket said. Had he made a mistake showing her his true form? Vivian said that she'd made peace with herself with the help of Addison's story, but she was only four and had already been immersed in stories of what Western unicorns were supposed to be. "Can I see yours?"

But Tara had gone shy and she bent to take the rope toy from the puppy.

Becket did what often served him well and sat down in the grass, wondering if he would regret it as he felt the cool damp through his pants. The puppy was sorely divided between the rope that Tara was holding and the allure of having a person down in licking range.

"I don't know much about kirin," he said invitingly. "Will you tell me?"

"I'm lucky," Tara said, trying to keep the puppy's attention. "Kirin are lucky. We have to go in."

Becket wasn't sure if it was foresight, luck, or just that they had been out there long enough for Vivian to get Shane to sleep, but the back sliding door opened then and Vivian called, "Tara, it's time for bed!"

Tara abandoned the puppy to bolt for the house. The puppy stopped to pick up the tug, tripped over it onto his face and rolled right back up, apparently forgetting all about the toy as he barreled for the door. Becket followed more sedately, stumbling over the threshold in the growing darkness.

"I'll get her down," Vivian said.

Becket was playing back his transformation in his mind, wondering what he should have done instead and how he was going to make it right again. He didn't want to fail Vivian at the only thing she'd asked of him.

But after they'd done the bathroom routine, Becket was surprised from his guilty rewind by Tara shyly bringing him a dog-eared pile of papers. "Will you read me?" she asked shyly.

This was her story, Becket realized at once, glancing over the loose pages. *The Kirin Who Could.*

"I would love to," he said genuinely, and he read it to her twice, all the way through, turning the pages carefully in his lap as she leaned against him and pointed herself out on the pages.

"That's me," she said, pointing to the sinuous brown unicorn with a dragon's face and scales, mobile whiskers on its muzzle. "I'm lucky."

"That's you," she said, pointing at the stallion of the herd of white unicorns.

Becket looked up and saw Vivian in the doorway, leaning against the frame with her arms wrapped around her, a contented smile on her face. "I kind of feel like I'm the lucky one," he said honestly.

CHAPTER 22

$\mathcal{A}$t that moment, Vivian was sure she was the luckiest one of all. Tara was drowsing against Becket, who was starting her book for the third time, without a word of complaint or impatience.

Vivian had already read it to her at least a thousand times, and as much as she loved the story, and that it had been made especially for her daughter, there were nights she would gladly have read War and Peace or a legal document or even Chicka-Chicka-Boom-Boom for the millionth time as a change of pace.

Hearing it in Becket's warm voice made it all new again, and the kirin's rescue of the unicorn herd seemed more poignant than ever.

He was a unicorn.

Vivian didn't think she believed in destiny. She was a practical woman and trusted in the concept of free will.

But what were the chances that she'd fall for two unicorns in her lifetime?

And what were the chances that she'd lose them both too soon?

Tara was asleep by the time he read the final words, and he put the loose pages reverently aside and gathered Tara up into his arms to follow Vivian into the little girl's bedroom and tuck her into her bed.

Becket kissed Vivian at Tara's closed door, and slowly down the hallway to her room, undressing as they went. Vivian didn't need or want words, only to slake the hunger that Becket had woken in her, to bury her fingers in his hair and draw him against her skin, all along her body.

Becket responded in kind, holding her so close that it was challenging to remove the last of their clothing, kissing her and reminding her without words how much he desired every curve and plane of her flesh. Vivian had no complaints or comparisons to make, only let herself enjoy every touch and brush of his mouth against her.

His cock was flatteringly hard and Vivian

knew that he was as on fire as she was and fighting back his own desire to prolong their pleasure by the way that he hissed and shuddered.

Vivian drew back and looked at him with challenge in her eyes. "Don't be gentle," she growled.

She didn't have to ask twice or explain herself.

She had forgotten his shifter strength, fooled by his gentleness and care, and she gave a little gasp as he tore off her last scrap of clothing and wrestled her to the bed.

She went willingly, spreading her legs as he lay her down and clawing at his magnificent shoulders. He took his own underwear off with even less finesse. He sucked at her neck—would she end up with a hickey like a horny teenager? Vivian didn't even care, she loved it so much, and then he was pressing his shaft into her without any further foreplay.

Vivian was shamelessly wet and eager, absolutely in the moment of pleasure and need with no reserve or restraint.

They coupled frantically and she writhed beneath his sexy weight and clawed the blankets beneath them into landscapes of ecstasy as he took her with ferocious intensity until her vision all but whited out with her release.

Then he was collapsing on her and pulling her close for his last frantic thrusts with a final moan of pleasure.

It was everything she had wanted and needed, no lingering or sightseeing along the way, just two bodies in the same quest for desperate sexual relief, bolstered by inexplicable trust and easy affection.

As her brain came back in the shuddering afterglow, Vivian still wasn't sure if she believed in fate, but she knew that the chances of randomly finding someone so perfectly attuned to her, so completely in step with her own desires and dreams, were so slim as to be impossible.

So why couldn't it be destiny?

CHAPTER 23

*I*t was so hard to sleep with Vivian.

She didn't snore or steal the blankets or kick him.

Becket simply didn't *want* to sleep, to waste any second of their time together on mundane needs like rest and food. He wanted to pleasure her sweet body long after they were both sated, far beyond the abilities of their flesh.

She seemed to feel the same way about him, and after they were finished and cleaned up, she fought back her exhaustion to lie with him and stroke his arms like he was a fractious animal.

How could she make him so endlessly content? How did she soothe all the restless anger out of him and somehow make everything absolutely perfect in their flawed, faulty lives?

"The day care that Tara goes to, is it for shifters only?" Any conversational topic would do, they often talked of trivialities, but this was a question that had been tickling at Becket's curiosity.

"Not just shifters. I can bring Shane there and there are a few other human kids, but it's for families of shifters, yes."

"I've never been in a town with so many shifters," Becket said, tracing the line of her neck, wishing he had the energy and stamina to do more. "I've never heard of a place that needed a day care for shifters."

"The family formula has changed with the times, too," Vivian pointed out. "There aren't so many extended units with grandparents and aunts available to watch children. Mothers don't always have the option to stay home anymore."

"Especially single mothers," Becket observed.

"*Especially* single mothers," Vivian agreed.

That led them on a conversational journey through talking about gender roles, laughing over the most ridiculous expectations as they fought off slumber.

"Jin's parents expected very traditional roles,"

Vivian told him. "They wanted me to give up my work and stay home when Tara was born and I was vehemently against that. Jin was a stay-at-home dad and I don't think they ever really forgave me for emasculating him that way, no matter how much he insisted that it was his own choice."

"Emasculating?" Becket snorted in outrage. "I've dealt with enough kids to know that the job of childcare is about a hundred times more demanding than nursing, and that's not a knock on nursing," he hastened to add. "I didn't mean to imply that at all."

"Dig yourself deeper, mister," Vivian teased. She sobered, then confessed, "I...never told them about Shane."

"They don't know about Shane?" Anything less than absolute honesty seemed out of character for Vivian.

"I feared that they only let us distance ourselves from them because Tara was a girl. I was terrified that they would, I don't know, stake some kind of claim on Shane, because he was a boy, declare me unfit, I don't even know. I wasn't obviously pregnant at his funeral and I just couldn't face dealing with that, *too*. I'm not proud of my choice, but I was desperate enough to make it at the time. And I've just…never gotten around to letting them know since then. They keep asking to see Tara, hinting about holidays together, but I've been putting them off."

"Sometimes, the path of least resistance actually is the best," Becket said, smoothing down her hair. "You don't *owe* them anything."

Vivian sighed. "I owe them the truth. They have a grandson, and Shane and Tara should know their grandparents. Mine certainly aren't interested. But it's not fair of me to keep them from grandparents who *are*, no matter how old-fashioned I think they are."

"If we got married, I would wash all of the dishes and change all the dirty diapers," Becket promised, only realizing after he said it that he definitely shouldn't have.

Marriage was *permanent* and Becket wasn't.

Til death do we part was altogether too poignant.

Vivian was quiet so long that Becket worried that she was angry with him, then looked down to realize that she had lost her battle with sleep at last. Her eyes were closed and her breath was slow and steady.

He gazed at her for as long as he could keep his eyes open, drinking in the freckles on her skin, her curves, the messy waves of her soft hair. Her face was even happy when it was slack, like she was reliving all her most joyous memories in her sleep.

Becket wanted to be in those joyous memories.

He wanted to be at her side, in her life, in a way that he'd never before craved. He could imagine settling here for good. If Nickel City had a broad enough shifter population to support a day care, it stood to reason they could support a doctor who could treat shifter children with their special needs. He longed to be a part of that community, to use his skills for them even if he couldn't use his magic.

He wanted to protect and provide forever.

And if he couldn't have forever, he could at least have now.

CHAPTER 24

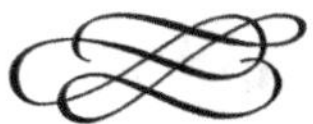

"Are you sure you want to do this?" Vivian asked skeptically. There was *amazing guy who would change dirty diapers and bathe babies*, and then there was just *dumb*. "There are going to be dozens of sugared up kids in itchy costumes wound up to eleven fighting over plastic spider rings and crying because they are overstimulated and exhausted. It is not a date. It doesn't even rhyme with date."

"I am absolutely sure," Becket said stoically. "I love Halloween!"

"You could stay home with the puppy," she suggested. "No one would blame you."

"But I've spent so long on my costume!" Becket protested.

Vivian had to giggle. He was wearing a long-sleeved black T-shirt and a pair of black pants, over which he had slung a secondhand size 3XL woman's white strappy slip. With a black Sharpie, he had written *Freudian* across the chest.

"It is clever," she had to agree. It was also admirably brave of him to wear women's underwear in public. The clients at the clinic had loved it, though Vivian thought that their male patients had perhaps appreciated the unexpected extra cleavage of her pirate shirt even more. She hadn't worn it in several Halloweens and it was definitely on the very edge of decent. She'd barely gotten the corset laced and had to skip the last holes altogether, but at least the jaunty neck scarf covered the hickey on her neck.

"Wouldn't you rather just hang here? We'll just make a token appearance and I'll be back in an hour."

"If you have to go, I will, too," Becket said firmly.

Part of being a widow was assuring everyone that she was still capable of getting out and Vivian's casual mom-friends had insisted that she bring the kids to a Halloween party being hosted by the Nickel City middle school. Vivian had brushed them off too many times lately to put them off again, even if she'd honestly rather trick or treat at one or two token local houses and make an early night of it.

The icy, slushy rain, threatening to turn entirely to snow, was the final kicker. It was too miserable to go house to house, and Tara had been hearing about Halloween from the other kids at Tiny Paws and was desperately invested in all the trappings.

"I'm a princess!" she crowed now, spinning in place. "I'm a princess! I'm a princess!"

"Okay, princess," Becket said, bending to scoop her up. "Where's your raincoat?" His slip gave a threatening creak. "Okay, I don't fold that way. How do you ladies manage this?"

Somehow, they all got to the car still mostly dry and Vivian drove them to the middle school. A tree out front was draped in sodden toilet paper and there were pumpkins all along the path to the gym doors. Their candles had been drenched in the rain.

The festival was everything that Vivian had promised it would be, noisy and chaotic, and she could not stop smiling. She introduced Becket to everyone she knew, and they all made noises of approval over his ridiculous costume and smirked knowingly at Vivian. "I'm going to have to hold them off with my sword," she joked with him when she'd rescued him from a particularly flirty single mom.

Tara wanted to try every game, taking her turn so slowly that kids behind her got impatient. She sank exactly no beanbags and didn't even hit the wall of balloons with her darts, but they gave her candy and prizes at every stop. Her eyes got bigger and bigger as her bag got heavy with sweets and toys, and she paused frequently to open it and crow over the colorful loot.

Shane, dressed in a lion sleeper, refused to wear his mane and spent most of the evening being passed back and forth between Vivian and Becket to try to forestall fussing.

As much as she'd tried to persuade Becket to stay behind—for his own good—Vivian was glad to have him along. It was far easier to manage a clingy four-year-old and a restless eight-month-old with four arms, and Vivian found it a welcome change to catch sidelong looks of envy instead of pity.

They ought to envy her, Vivian thought. Becket was by far the best-looking man in the building, and he was clearly there for her support, not a shred of reluctance or embarrassment as he unwrapped candy and held Tara's tiara, sometimes even wearing it. He helped Tara as much as Vivian did, and had Shane at least half the time. He didn't look as harried or put-out as most of the other dads, and he was cheerful and patient.

None of the kids got his costume.

"Are you an angel?" a little girl guessed.

"Are you a girl?" her older brother asked.

"I'm a Freudian slip," Becket explained.

They looked at him blankly.

"Is that a TV show?"

Their parents got it about half the time and mostly laughed, though there were a few who only looked appalled.

"This isn't nearly as bad as you advertised," Becket said, bouncing Shane on his hip as they waited for Tara to pick a consolation prize for failing to get rings on a bottle.

Vivian smiled around. It was loud and wild, but for the most part they were shrieks of laughter, not outrage, and she thought it was well-managed for the number of hyper children. Some of the older kids were climbing on the folded up bleachers, pushing each other and daring each other to jump.

"The night is young," she cautioned.

On cue, over the laughter and chatter, there was suddenly a scream of alarm and one of the middle school children fell from the bleachers where they were wrestling. There was a sickening crunch when they hit the floor, and Vivian didn't think it was only the sound of a costume being crushed.

CHAPTER 25

Becket's instinct gave a flare of alarm and he shoved Shane at Vivian without thinking so that he was free to bolt through the crowd to the fallen child.

"I'm a doctor!" he explained, pushing his way through the fringe of children and parents who had gathered to gape.

The youth, a boy of about thirteen dressed as a Power Ranger, was silent but writhing in pain, holding the arm that he'd fallen on and gritting his teeth. The other kids who'd been with him were doing plenty of screaming and crying for him.

Becket glanced up at the height of the bleachers and tried to guess how he'd come down on the arm. It was a nasty fall, if not life-threatening, but it looked like he'd been unlucky in landing. The forearm or wrist was almost certainly broken, and not cleanly.

There was a tingle of recognition as he got closer and Becket knew this was a shifter. "Let me see," he commanded, and the closest kids drew back obediently as Becket knelt beside him, hearing stitches pop in his slip as he did. "I'm not exactly dressed for this," he admitted jovially, "but I promise I'm a doctor. I work at the Nickel City Family Clinic, do you know it?"

The boy grimaced and jerked his head, but looked like he didn't dare unlock his jaw. His nostrils were flared and he was panting through his teeth. He lay still while Becket gently took his arm in his hands and Becket felt him shudder in agony.

And no wonder.

Becket's unicorn hissed in sympathy. *Broken,* he agreed. *Here, and here, and here.*

It was the kind of messy break that would almost certainly require surgery. And surgery for shifter children was deeply complicated, given their quicker-than-expected recovery rate. It also tended to require a lot of blood tests that would give alarming results under scrutiny, with high indicators of problems that didn't exist for them. It would raise a lot of questions, if nothing else, and lead his parents on a merry and expensive medical chase, putting all of them under suspicion.

"Should we call 9-1-1?" one of the older kids asked. A few parents had their phones out and looked indecisive.

"It's probably just sprained," Becket lied convincingly. "Let me see."

He looked up to see Vivian catch him in the falsehood. She had Shane on one hip and Tara by the other hand. "Is there anything I can do?" she offered without judgment as she let go of Tara and knelt opposite him. "What's your name, kiddo?"

The boy only grunted as one of his friends volunteered, "Darius. His name is Darius."

"Hi, Darius," Vivian said gently. "You're in good hands with Doctor Becket. Can we get a little space here, please?"

Did she know what he planned to do? The kids and parents drew obediently back at her firm words, and Becket took advantage of the attention being briefly on her to flow in with his unicorn and inspect the injury.

How much? he asked with trepidation. *How much would it take?*

He couldn't think about the cost of his magic without being keenly aware of Vivian, just across from him. Even hindered by Shane, she was his perfect partner, deflecting all the attention away so that he could do his work. She was so selfless and serene and just her presence had settled the crowd around them. The children were less upset, the parents less pushy and panicked.

She was everything he had ever wanted. She was kind and beautiful and sexy and smart. She made him laugh and feel alive the way he'd somehow lost without ever being aware of it. The pirate costume flattered her curvy figure and made him want to dive into her cleavage right there in front of everyone.

Becket forced himself back to the job at hand.

Knitting bones was tricky. Flesh was more eager to seal back together, but the skeleton was slow to react, sluggish and sedate in its healing.

His unicorn considered, prodding at the future. *A week,* he finally said. *A week if we do only the bones.*

Becket couldn't refuse the boy a week of his own life to protect his secret and save him so much suffering. He reluctantly looked at Vivian, who was murmuring comforting things to Darius and touching his back to divert him from the pain as she gazed knowingly back at Becket.

Shane, bored by his mother's inattention, gave a squawk and tried to lean forward out of her grasp. Vivian caught him and Becket used the distraction as an opportunity, closing his eyes and sending his unicorn's magic through his fingertips into Darius.

If it had been a showy kind of power, full of the glitter and sparkle and rainbows usually associated with unicorns, he would have had no chance to help the boy with the audience they had. But all that anyone watching carefully might have seen was a slight twitch of the arm he was holding as he pulled all the shards of bone into place beneath the muscles, and forced them to weld back together. Darius arched in pain, hissing in between his bared teeth, and Becket wrestled with his impulse to block his receptors and spare him that suffering. He wanted to use as little magic as possible, and leave the damage convincing. He couldn't afford to draw attention to them by making the pain vanish or orchestrating a miraculous healing.

Vivian pulled the whole thing off as if Shane's struggle was the cause of Darius's sudden agony.

"Don't touch, baby!" she murmured, pulling him back into her arms. "Let's be more careful!"

"Is he okay?" A woman dressed as Elvira with long black hair and a shifter tingle knelt down beside Vivian.

Finished just in time, Becket nodded. "I'm pretty sure it's just a sprain," he said, trying not to sound out of breath. "He should have it X-rayed, just in case. Are you his mother?"

She chuckled dryly. "No, just his science teacher, Olivia. We've…met."

It took Becket that long to recognize her, because something had drastically changed. Underneath the dramatic goth makeup was the woman he'd found with the catatonic shifter earlier that fall in a suddenly extinguished forest fire that he'd never been able to completely explain to himself. He thought she hadn't been a shifter then, and she clearly was now, in a sense that she was more sizzling than tingling. Becket had never heard of someone so old coming into shifter powers; clearly he must misremember their first meeting.

"How are you feeling, Darius?" Olivia asked after sharing a knowing look with Becket.

"I can wiggle my fingers," the boy said hoarsely, finally able to unlock his jaw.

Olivia helped him sit up. "We'll call your dad and get you to the ER for that scan," she said, reaching for a phone. "I don't think this requires an ambulance. But maybe this will convince you that you *can't* fly."

Darius looked alarmed and glanced around at the closest people, cradling his arm to his body. Becket knew that it would continue to hurt wickedly for some time. He hadn't done a thing to help the abused flesh around the bones, but an X-ray would show only tissue damage now, and the boy should be able to avoid invasive surgery and investigation. He'd get a brace and heal the rest of the way as normal.

As normally as any shifter healed, anyway.

The doctor who took the case would probably guess that he'd overestimated the injury when it was completely good in just a few weeks. Sprains and strains were hard to quantify at the best of times. There wouldn't be any lingering mystery.

Exhaustion suddenly swamped him and Becket had to resist the urge to lie down on the cold gym floor and go to sleep.

The crowd was slowly dispersing, the celebratory mood of the Halloween festival greatly dampened by the accident. Kids went to get the last of the candy and prizes and parents tried to herd them to the exits. Olivia got Darius upright and led him away, his friends trailing anxiously behind them.

"Are you okay?" Vivian asked in a low voice. She got to her feet, hampered by a struggling Shane and a clinging Tara, and offered him a hand that Becket was alarmed to find that he needed.

Healing was always tiring, but this seemed extreme. He felt like he'd just run a marathon, or lifted an impossible number of weights.

"I'm fine," he said. "Fine. Just need a little rest." He could taste the lie in his mouth. His heart was straining in his chest, making it hard to breathe, and he had to concentrate to keep his head up and his body from shaking.

"Let's go," Vivian commanded, clearly not fooled. "Tara, we need to find the stroller and get your coat on. We have candy at home, you don't need more prizes."

Becket followed her, careful to keep from staggering, smiling his best at everyone.

CHAPTER 26

Becket's big smile didn't fool Vivian for a moment.

With the assistance of experience, she juggled Tara and Shane and the stroller out into the cold twilight. The rain had turned to snow in earnest, so the stroller had to be hauled along through the slush to the car, and it took much longer than usual to get both children buckled into their car seats. Becket, who always helped with this process, tried to protest when she opened the passenger seat for him first and commanded that he sit down.

"I could—"

"Don't argue," Vivian told him. "I'm in better shape than you right now, and I will totally win."

"I can—"

"Sit!"

Becket sat.

Tara climbed into her car seat and let Vivian buckle her in after Shane was secured. The stroller was folded up in the back.

The drive home was hairy and slow, not helped by very determined trick-or-treaters who had no respect for traffic laws, or the wet sleet underneath the fluffy topping of snow. Vivian found her attention divided between driving and wanting to check Becket's pulse as he sat listlessly beside her. Every so often, he would look over and give her a smile she thought he meant as reassuring.

Getting everyone out of the car and into the house was as much work as getting there and Vivian didn't have time to be alarmed by Becket's clear exhaustion until she'd let the puppy out to pee, gotten Shane down to sleep, and herded a wound-up Tara into the bathroom.

Becket was slumped on the couch, covered in Tara's princess cloak, with her tiara perched on his head. "Sorry I'm not more help," he said, voice slurred like he was drunk.

Vivian sat on what was left of the couch and he leaned on her. The puppy whined at their feet and tried unsuccessfully to hop up on the couch with them, finally settling for lying across her shoes when she refused to pick him up.

"You healed that boy," she said, glancing at the shut bathroom door. Tara was humming and taking her sweet time.

"It was riskier not to," Becket said stubbornly. "That break would have required surgery, and he was a shifter. I had to help protect his secrets."

"What did it cost?" Vivian asked, not sure if she wanted to actually know.

Becket hesitated so long that she thought that he wasn't going to answer. Then he sighed. "A week. Give or take."

A week.

They'd known each other almost exactly that long.

And it had been a glorious week. A week of falling so hard in love that Vivian wasn't sure what would happen when she hit the bottom. *Was* there a bottom?

If she'd been given a choice, would she have traded *this* week to protect someone else? Vivian was not sure she was that strong.

"Is it always like this?" Vivian wanted to know, tucking the cloak in around him tenderly. "Are you this tired every time?"

"It's work," Becket said with a tiny shrug. "*Hard* work. This one was kind of tricky, but I'll be fine after I've rested. I promise." He took her hand in his and squeezed it.

Vivian let herself take some comfort from his words and from his fingers, then rose to her feet to get Tara moving along to bed, the puppy scrambling to keep up with her.

Tara had taken her bag of treats into the bathroom with her and upended them onto the bathroom rug, where she was sitting sorting through them. The puppy frolicked into the center of the loot, to Tara's dismay, picked up the largest candy bar, and bolted back out of the bathroom.

"Oh, not chocolate!" Vivian said. "It will make him sick!"

She wasn't sure if Tara's outraged wail was because her treats had been stolen, because she was afraid for the puppy, or if she was just generally worn out from their exciting Halloween adventures, but it was enough to warn the puppy that this was something beyond their usual play. He bounded out into the living room and wiggled into a space behind the couch that Vivian hadn't even known he could fit. Here, he crouched down and growled around the candy in his mouth.

It was a playful growl, and Vivian could hear his tail thumping against the couch.

She tried coaxing him out with both promises and threats, tried laying down and blindly grasping for him until she was pretty sure she'd wrenched her shoulder.

Finally, Becket stood to help her pull the couch away from the wall so that she could reach over the back and pull him up by the scruff of the neck, glad that he wasn't any larger than he was.

"Bad dog!" she said, prying the prize from his stubborn jaws. He'd chewed through the wrapper, but there wasn't a dangerous amount of chocolate gone. What was left was a slobbery, sticky mess, and the puppy was wearing a fair portion of it.

Becket, nearly swaying in exhaustion, threw away the bar for her and brought her a fistful of damp paper towels to wipe as much of it off as she could before it was licked off by eager puppy tongue.

The sunny-natured puppy thought this was a wonderful part of the game, whining happily at all of the attention. Tara was crying, and Becket went to comfort her and help put all her candy and toys safely back in her bag.

When she finally thought that the puppy

wasn't going to leave chocolate pawprints all over her house, Vivian released him, and he went scampering after Tara, who promptly forgave him and wanted to give him treats. Vivian could tell that Becket was fading fast, so she steered him to the askew couch and sat him back down. "You don't have to be a superhero all the time," she reminded him with a kiss on the forehead.

"I think you're the one who usually needs that reminder," he countered with a grateful smile.

"Do as I say, not as I do!"

"Can the puppy sleep with me?" Tara begged, the way she did every night.

"No, sweetie," Vivian said. "The puppy sleeps in his own bed."

She let Tara give the puppy a consolation treat, giggling as she got licked all over, then, after another detour to the bathroom, finally got her into bed.

"I have to pee," Tara said sleepily.

"You just peed."

"I need a drink."

"You got a drink in the bathroom."

"I'm thirsty."

"Are you sure?"

Tara snuggled deeper into her blankets and

Vivian thought she might be able to escape at last. She stood carefully, not wanting to alarm Tara.

"Don't go!" Tara cried. "Hug!"

"Hand hug," Vivian countered, taking her hand for a quick clasp.

Tara clung to her for a moment, then let Vivian tuck her hand back under the covers.

Vivian closed the door behind her as quietly as she could and stood there in the hallway a moment to see if she would be called back once again.

She came out to find that Becket had tipped over on the couch and the puppy had either managed to scramble up or Becket had lifted him up to snuggle into his arms. The puppy was lying still, but his eyes were open and his tail wagged sheepishly when he caught sight of Vivian.

Becket was already asleep, taking up the entire couch, and Vivian sucked in her breath and sank down on the floor next to them.

The puppy squirmed just enough to reach her with his cold nose and lick her ear. Vivian stroked his soft little head and his eyes closed blissfully.

Then everyone else was asleep and the house was quiet except for the hum of the refrigerator and the creak of the baseboard heat.

Vivian let her eyes close for a moment, re-living the evening in wonder.

It wasn't that she hadn't believed that Becket could magically heal people, or known what it cost him, but witnessing it drove home all the improbable parts of it.

Sometimes, she felt like she was walking on a narrow ledge between the ordinary world of diapers and deadlines and one of magic and enchantment, where people could change into animals and work miracles. It took such careful balance, with one foot in each world, but she could not imagine anything more wondrous.

And what a burden, she thought, looking at Becket's dear face, slack in sleep. What a wretched choice it must be, every single time, to decide to help someone at the expense of his own life.

It hurt to know that she would lose Becket that much sooner for saving Darius a pile of grief and pain, and sparing his family the curiosity and suspicion that would have followed his injury if Becket had done what sense suggested.

Vivian smiled, smoothing a spare lock of his hair back from his handsome cheek. Becket could have done nothing less, she knew, and it was a huge part of what she loved about him. He was selfless and warm-hearted, exactly what she wanted in a life partner.

Whatever life they had together.

She was glad to have the time she could have with him, to treasure every moment.

What would the world be like, Vivian wondered, if shifters didn't have to be secret?

Could they ever live in open harmony with the ordinary? Or would jealousy and fear prevail? She hated to think that prejudice would win, but she feared it would, and she knew enough history and current events to know that people who were afraid and felt powerless were dangerous. It was better, for now, to keep their abilities hidden, to stay quietly in the shadows.

Vivian was tired, but she knew that she wasn't capable of moving the slumbering doctor, and she didn't want to leave him for any of the precious moments they had left, so she snagged a throw with her foot and snuggled down where she was, the puppy snoring evenly near her ear, Becket's breath in her hair. She had slept in more uncomfortable positions over her years as a mother.

She dreamed of a green grassy field full of

flowers, Tara in her kirin form romping with a gleaming white unicorn, and cried with joy in her sleep.

CHAPTER 27

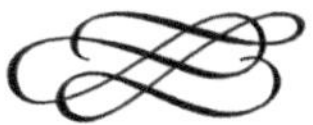

"We're not naming the puppy," Vivian insisted, every morning, as if she could use his namelessness to deny his entrance to their family. "We're still looking for his owners!"

But by that night, whether from Tara, Becket, Crystal, or the other nurses, he had worn at least three names.

"His name is Buttercup," Tara said this evening. She was on the floor on all fours, barking and trying to teach him how to shake. Becket had brought a bag of training treats, but they were being ignored in favor of licking and playing with Tara. He wore his collar now, pink woven nylon with a blank name tag in the shape of a bone and a rabies tag.

"Sit!" Tara said. "Sit! Shake! No!"

The puppy fell over on his side, wiggling and panting happily, and Tara tried to haul him back up to sitting. "Sit!"

The puppy pretended to have no bones, melting against Tara as she struggled to get him upright, and Vivian thought that it was only fair that Tara have to deal with that after all of her sudden leg collapses when she wasn't getting her way on a shopping trip.

"Here," Becket offered. He crawled down off the couch onto the floor with them and took the treat from Tara. "Hold it up high like this. Sit!" he told the puppy, dragging the treat past his nose into the air. The puppy stood up and strained for it as Becket put a hand at the base of his tail and pressed. "Sit!"

The puppy obediently sat and Tara crowed in triumph. "Now praise him," Becket told her, handing over the treat.

"Good doggy! Good Buttercup!"

"We're not naming the dog," Vivian said helplessly.

Tara fed not-Buttercup the coveted treat and the canine turned to investigate Tara's pocket for more, making her squeal and giggle. "Shake!" she cried, trying to catch the puppy's paw. "Shake! Sit!"

They both fell over instead, in a happy wriggling heap.

Becket scooted to the couch so that he was sitting next to Vivian's feet and smiled up at her. He was so handsome and happy, and Vivian leaned forward to kiss the crown of his head. Shane was in her lap and he gave a squawk of protest at being squished and took a handful of Becket's hair when it was in reach.

"Ow, what a grip!" Becket said without anger, and when he reached up to take Shane into his own lap, Vivian didn't even have that moment of alarm that she always had to squash passing him off to someone else. It was as natural and safe as if…

Vivian forced herself to examine her reaction.

She felt like Becket belonged.

He belonged in her heart, and in her family.

How was she supposed to reconcile this with the knowledge that their time together was short?

The answer to that was surprisingly simple, as she sat and looked over her cozy living room.

Tara was throwing a ball for the puppy Vivian was nearly ready to name, her aim and strength enthusiastic but absolutely terrible. The puppy's pursuit of it was nearly as bad, and he skidded into sturdy furniture and ricocheted off with the enviable resilience of youth, then came dancing back to tease Tara with the ball that he wouldn't give up without a fight.

Becket sat at Vivian's feet, leaning just a little on one of her legs as he played nonsense games with Shane on his knees. "Who's dancing? Who's dancing? Shane's dancing! Don't fall! I've got you!"

Shane chortled in joy, his chubby face in a wide, drooly grin as he bounced in place, clinging to Becket's hands and testing his newly discovered knees.

What else could Vivian do but treasure every moment of this gift?

All happiness ended eventually, in any life with mortality, and if she had the rather uncomfortable advantage of knowing, nearly exactly, when Becket's did, it only meant that she needed to appreciate the time that she had with him more than ever.

Jin had known that, she realized, and the tears that welled up in her eyes against her will were bittersweet.

He had lived completely, loved without reservation, and given them every advantage and affection that he could manage before he faced his fate, never letting the shadow of it darken their days. Vivian had always marveled at his ability to let frustrations wash over him, at his patience and acceptance of speed bumps and disappointments. She'd never actually understood how strong his heart really was.

And she hadn't realized how much she'd learned from his example, or how much she would need it now.

Becket was stroking her calf and looking up at her, Shane swaying drunkenly in his lap. "You okay?" he asked quietly.

Vivian blinked and wiped the tears that escaped her eyes with the back of a hand. "I'm okay," she said honestly. "It's a lot sometimes, but I'm *glad* you're here."

She knew that she would grieve hard for Becket when he left them, that her heart was already committed, but she refused to borrow that sorrow early. "I'm glad you're here," she repeated, bending to kiss his forehead. "Let's get the kids to bed."

Tara looked up in alarm, caught in the act of rubbing her eyes. "I'm not sleepy!" she protested.

"Puppies need sleep!" Vivian said. "It's time for us to put the puppy to bed!"

The puppy growled and shook the ball in his mouth so hard that he nearly fell over.

"Can he sleep with me?" Tara begged.

"The puppy has to sleep in his own bed," Vivian told her firmly.

"But he's lonely and he cries!"

"All babies do at first," Vivian reminded her. The hardest part about the crate training was the heartbreak of separation. "Let's take him outside so he can go potty, just like you do before bed."

"I'll give Shane a bath and get him dressed for bed," Becket offered, standing with Shane and giving the baby a little toss that made him shriek in joy.

Again, Vivian didn't have a moment of hesitation. He'd been there enough evenings now to know the routine, and she loved how he stepped up to accept whichever duties needed doing, however messy they might be. "Thank you. We'll be back soon," she said, pausing to give him a kiss. "Tara, do you want the flashlight or the leash?"

Vivian tucked a doggy bag into her windbreaker pocket as Tara caught the puppy and laboriously tried to clip the leash onto his collar.

The clasp was too stiff for her fingers. "I'll do that, darling. You get into your coat."

Although the Halloween snow had melted away in a few days, it was starting to frost at night. The air was brisk and Vivian was glad that she'd insisted they wear hats. She wished she'd thought to wear gloves as well. Tara swiftly gave up both flashlight and leash in order to put her hands in her pockets as they walked along the road towards an empty lot where they could loiter while the puppy did his business.

Tara ranged ahead at the end of the leash with the puppy, and Vivian put the flashlight in her pocket so she had at least one warm hand, watching them walk together. There were enough streetlights that she didn't fear losing them or their way. The flashlight was mostly for Tara's entertainment, and for finding the puppy's leavings to pick up.

The two tangled in the leash several times, and Vivian had to stop and unwind her giggling daughter.

They warmed up along the walk, and after the puppy had left a few piddles and a small steaming pile that Vivian scooped up in a bag and threw away, they turned and wandered back along a different block, Tara's hand in her own. They were both wearing out. The puppy was happy to trot along beside them, and Tara leaned more and more on Vivian's hand and slowed down until Vivian finally paused and picked her up.

"I like Docker Becket," Tara said unexpectedly, her voice sleepy. She was still holding her head upright, but Vivian knew it was only a matter of time before she was carrying an unconscious four-year-old and possibly a puppy—he was starting to stagger and was no longer pausing to sniff anything.

"I like Doctor Becket, too," Vivian said honestly.

"Will he go away like Daddy?" Tara asked. "He might have to."

As hard as Vivian had tried to brace herself for this conversation, she was not prepared for it, and she clutched hard at Tara and stumbled over a crack in the sidewalk she hadn't seen in the dark.

"He will, someday," Vivian said as gently as she could manage. A year was a long time when you'd only lived four of them. Someday was as specific as she needed to get.

"I'll miss him," Tara said thoughtfully.

Vivian squeezed her harder. "I will, too. But we'll have fun with him while we can."

"Just like Daddy," Tara said contentedly, laying her head against Vivian's shoulder.

CHAPTER 28

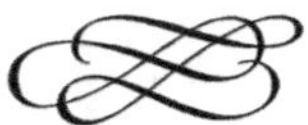

Shane was a remarkably happy baby, Becket thought.

He was full of wide-eyed observation of the world, joyful babble, and some really amazingly awful output.

"How can you be this delighted by something this vile?" Becket asked, wiping him down before the bath.

Shane only chortled, waving his fists and grabbing after the bottle of wipes.

"Thank you, at least, for doing this before your bath," Becket said, pausing to blow a raspberry on his bare belly.

Shane shrieked and laughed and kicked his legs, and Becket took him to splash in the inflatable bath inside the bathtub itself. He was sitting up reliably now, and by the time Vivian returned with Tara and the puppy she refused to name, Becket was as wet as he was.

"One bathed baby," Becket said, bringing him out of the bathroom wrapped in a towel. "Approximately two pounds lighter and less smelly than when you left."

"Oh, good timing," Vivian said. Tara was drowsing on her shoulder and the puppy took two steps into the house and flopped over on his side. "Why don't I trade you and I'll go nurse him a bit and get him down."

They made an awkward exchange, a limp Tara for a squirming Shane, and Vivian vanished into Shane's bedroom while Becket tried to balance getting Tara awake enough to brush her teeth and dress for bed without winding her up too much. She was asleep before he'd finished reading her a short book.

He and Vivian met on the couch a short time later and collapsed next to each other.

"The puppy should go in the crate," Vivian said, making no move to get up and make it happen.

"I have something I should tell you," Becket said regretfully.

"Is it worse than 'I have less than a year to live?'" Vivian wanted to know. How could she be so light-hearted and forward about it? Becket marveled at her strength of spirit.

He considered his answer. "It's probably not worse," he decided.

Vivian sat up and looked at him gravely. "Spill it."

Becket pursed his lips. "I haven't told you a lot about my childhood."

"You mentioned that your home life wasn't great as a child," Vivian said diplomatically. They had each shared memories of cool and uncaring parents but preferred to keep their conversation to happier topics.

"I always thought my dad drank because he could not handle the responsibilities of being a unicorn," he said. "I thought I could do better, when I was young and cocky. I wasn't always careful about my healing powers. I thought I was invincible, because I knew when I'd die, and I was…kind of reckless about trying to be a hero."

"This doesn't shock me," Vivian said. Her smile suggested that she liked that about him.

"I got caught, once."

Vivian sobered. "Like, literally caught?"

"I wish—oh, I wish!—that everyone in the

world was like you," Becket said honestly. "But there are people who see magic and they want that power for themselves. They want to use it, to control it, to sell it."

"Who was it? What did they do?"

"I'd fixed a guy's heart problem—it was kind of an easy thing, just kind of cleared out some grime, really, and he was blabbing about it. I felt really good, like I could be famous, but he told a friend, who told a friend, and a man named Hunter tracked me down, though he had a pretty wild version of the story."

"Like that telephone game."

Becket smiled wryly. "Okay, so here's the embarrassing part. I trusted him. I trusted that he could help me use my powers in the best possible way. Hunter ran a super exclusive medical and research center, with only the richest clients and all the best equipment. It wasn't really…aboveboard, or accredited, but it was the very best of the best. I was really impressed, and we were going to be a team. He was going to find me patients that I could save, the best use of my power, the most need. He'd be able to screen them, so I wasn't wasting my time on scraped knees and pedestrian colds. I knew that otherwise, I'd have to go get my own medical degree, become a doctor myself, so I could help people without magic. That seemed like way too much work at that age."

"But you did, later. You have a real degree, now. That can't have been easy." Vivian was listening with her whole body, her legs curled up underneath her.

"It would have been better if I'd done that up front," Becket said. "Hunter lied to me and used me. He strung me along, told me what to do and who to heal, and let me believe that I was a hero."

"What happened?"

"I was pushing to help more people, to do things like cure cancer at homeless shelters and help poor people, not just rich people. When we argued, I realized that he didn't want to do that, that he only cared about what he could *get* for my healing. This is also when I realized what it was costing me."

"In time."

"In life," Becket agreed. "It was like I could see ahead along a string of my destiny, and there was an *end* to it that I could see coming. Like a wall. Or a knot."

"Did you tell him?"

"Yes. At first, I think that he just didn't believe me. I was sixteen, a runaway. He probably figured that I'd gotten bored and was looking for a way out of our arrangement. He started getting more aggressive about making me do things, looking for ways to leverage me. At first, it was all good stuff, money, a fancy car, cool things I'd never had as a kid. But you'd be surprised how fast the shine wears off. After a while, he realized that he could use innocent people to blackmail me. He'd let me cure some poor kid's cancer if I fixed some old rich guy's lung disease. It only got uglier from there. I figured out that he wasn't above hurting people to control me, and I saw how fast my end was coming because he kept making me do more and more."

"But you got away from him. You're a legitimate doctor."

"I got away. I changed my name again and started over clean. I wanted to heal people, and if I couldn't do it with magic—without consequence—I was going to figure out how to do it the hard way instead."

"Has it been difficult not to use it?" Vivian asked knowingly.

"It is sometimes the hardest part of my life," Becket confessed. "Knowing that I could make something painless and fast, but letting a person do it the long, agonizing way. Sometimes, I can sort of slide in there and help things along without too much cost, but a minute here and a day there adds up at the end."

How did he explain the endless push-pull of such a double-edged power? He wanted to save people suffering, and at the same time, he wanted to hoard what was left of his finite ability and live as long as he had left. Especially now, with Vivian and her children sharing his heart.

"You're bringing this up now for a reason, aren't you." Vivian didn't say it like a question. "Instinct?"

"Instinct," Becket agreed. "It's a feeling I've had for a few days now, just a kind of a nagging concern with no particular direction, remembering those times that I hadn't thought of in years. My unicorn is restless. And it's gotten stronger, just today. I was hoping that it had been long enough that Hunter wasn't even looking for me anymore, but I've learned to listen to these worries and I wanted to warn you."

Vivian was quiet. Did she guess the parts that Becket hadn't confessed, the parts that he hated to think of the most? She might not be a shifter, but she sometimes had an understanding of people that was almost supernatural.

If she suspected that he was withholding details from her, she gave no indication of it.

"If he comes looking for you again, he'll have to get through me," she said with a smile that warmed his heart. "And our ferocious watchdog." She rubbed the sleeping puppy with one gentle foot and he groaned in his sleep.

CHAPTER 29

Vivian wasn't terribly surprised that there was another shoe, or that it had dropped at last. It was hard to trust that happiness could last—especially when she already knew that it wouldn't.

"Is it inappropriate of me to picture a stone basement mad scientist lab with Van Der Graaf generators and a whole lot of technicolor test tubes?" she asked, glad to see Becket's mouth curve up.

"Not inappropriate at all, though it was actually an upper story private condo with a whole lot of ultramodern equipment. It's less Adams Family and more Martha Stewart but medical."

"I suppose even evil geniuses have to stay up

with the times," Vivian said, nodding sagely. "I tell you, if I was going to be a supervillain, I'd totally lean into the aesthetics of it. Do they at least wear black leather?"

"Plenty of black leather," Becket assured her. "You're taking this really well."

"Becket," Vivian said frankly. "I married a fortune-telling unicorn who knew he was going to die. My daughter is a kirin who foretold the coming of a puppy that I swore we'd never get. My breastfeeding son has four sharp teeth and my boyfriend has a ticking countdown on his heart. If I could not roll with punches by now, I'd have lain down in my own grave already. An evil medical lab is just laughable on top of everything else I have to deal with."

"You are amazing," Becket said, sounding genuinely awed.

"I am a mother. I do six impossible things before breakfast every day."

"Is getting out of bed one of those?"

"I will admit that's gotten even harder since you started staying over," Vivian said with a sly smile.

"Harder, you say?" He kissed her when she tipped her face up to him, but she didn't indulge in more.

"What do we have to do to stay off their radar?" she asked when he had released her lips. "Do they know who you really are?"

"They only knew my…ah…pseudonym."

"You were working for them under an assumed name?"

"Y-yes…" Vivian didn't need supernatural senses to know that Becket was embarrassed by it. He was literally squirming next to her. It was adorable.

"You have to tell me now!" she exclaimed, turning to tickle him. "I must know! You wouldn't look like that if it wasn't truly terrible."

"I'll never confess!" Becket protested, laughing and catching her hands.

"Was it a unicorn name? Were you Sparkle Happy Dance? No, Rainbow Jewelheart!" Vivian slipped free of his grasp and got a hand around to catch him at the waist and tickle mercilessly.

"Vixen! Torturer! It will go to the grave with me!"

"Your grave isn't that far off, Starburst Suntwinkle! I'll torment it from your gorgeous lips before you go!"

Awoken by their playful struggle, the puppy jerked to his feet and scampered over to take part in the fun, whining and planting his paws on their knees before scrambling right up to try to squeeze in between them and lick everything he could reach.

"Ah! The tongue! The puppy will be my undoing! I am overcome!"

Becket actually slipped off of the couch, dragging both dog and Vivian with him, and she collapsed on top of him and got her face thoroughly licked before she could untangle herself and sit up out of reach again, laughing until tears streamed down her face.

"How can we laugh over this?" Becket asked in wonder, when they'd caught their breath again and the puppy was rolling on his back over his legs, chewing gently on his hand.

"Because if we don't laugh, we'll cry, and this is a lot more fun," Vivian told him seriously. "Becket, I love you. I even love all of your problems and your crazy superhero baggage because it's part of who you are. We'll get through this like we get through everything, making the best of whatever we have while we can."

The puppy was unceremoniously dumped from Becket's lap as he rose to his knees so that he could face Vivian and take her cheeks in his hands.

"Yes," he said simply. "Yes. I love you."

And then he kissed her, so hard that Vivian thought her lips would bruise, and she tangled her fingers in his hair and kissed him back.

The puppy, sure that this was more of the game, wriggled up in between them, sharp puppy claws clamoring at their arms as he whined and panted and wagged his tail furiously.

"What do we do to protect the kids?" Vivian asked at last, gathering the puppy into her arms and cuddling him close. "Should I keep them home from day care?" She couldn't think of a way to do that and still pay bills. It was hard enough balancing the two as it was.

Becket shook his head and put an easy arm around her. "I don't think they can be any safer than they are there. But I should—"

"I swear to God, Becket, if you suggest staying away from us for our protection I will end you early myself." The puppy in her arms squirmed and Vivian scratched his belly, sending him into raptures of limp delight.

"It would be safer," Becket protested.

"Living life isn't about the safest thing to do," Vivian said firmly. "Do you take stupid risks for no gain? Of course not, but I'm also not going to live a life pining over things I can't have when the only reason I couldn't have them is fear."

"I'm not saying we shouldn't see each other," Becket said. "I'm just saying that maybe we should be more…discrete."

"I'm pretty sure Crystal knows we're sleeping together," Vivian said wryly, playing with the puppy's paws. He was falling asleep again, his head lolling, in that amazing way that small creatures of all kinds could conk out at the drop of a coin. "And if Crystal knows, everyone knows. It wouldn't take Sherlock Holmes to figure us out. Are you afraid they'll use us for leverage to get to you, or do you think they'll figure out what Tara is and try to take her away?"

"I don't know," Becket said with admirable honesty. "I just don't want to put you in any danger. Ever."

Vivian set the boneless puppy aside and went to crawl into Becket's lap, straddling him and taking his face in her hands. "I am a grown woman and I get to decide what risks I'm willing to take. You are a risk I'm willing to take, even with your evil mad scientist black leather clad villains and your pending expiration date. Now kiss me, because I am not going to spend the rest of this night thinking about all the things that could go wrong when there's at least one thing that could go really, really right."

Becket was very willing to do exactly that, and he took her by the hand and led her to the bedroom, laying her down on the bed to coax every pleasure and passion from her that she'd somehow forgotten she might have. He filled her so deliciously, and carried her on waves so beautiful that she stopped keeping track of the peaks, and she cried out his name and clawed his shoulders as her world narrowed to their joyful joining.

Afterwards, they lay languidly together, still drinking in the feeling of flesh and fellowship until Vivian's skin began to goosebump.

"You never told me your nom de plume," she remembered, rising to get her bathrobe for a swift shower.

"It's worse than anything you guessed," Becket said. He was so beautiful, sprawled spent across her bed. He was golden, like a lion, lanky and deliciously fit, with dark hair curling over his skin in all the right places. Even so recently sated, he did something primal to Vivian's libido and she was sorely tempted to go crawling back to him for more.

"Well, you have to tell me now," she protested. "How bad can it be?"

"It's Philip."

"Philip? That's a great name. Isn't there a prince with that name?"

"Philip Singlehorn."

Vivian gave an ungraceful snort of surprise and delight. "Philip Singlehorn? Like...a unicorn?"

"I was young," Becket said, hiding his face in a pillow. "I thought it was clever."

Vivian laughed all the way to the shower, and swiftly rinsed off.

When she returned, she found the puppy had begged his way up onto the bed and was snuggled down with Becket, who looked guilty, but didn't offer to go put him in the crate. She didn't want to be the bad guy after such a lovely, full night, so Vivian only slipped in behind him, whispering a dire warning, "If he pees in the bedding, you're washing it."

CHAPTER 30

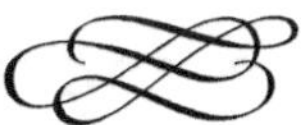

Fortunately, the puppy (named Treasure for a brief period that morning) did not pee on the bed, though there was a small accident on the floor that Becket cleaned up while Vivian was still sleeping. They arrived at the clinic separately, and Becket left the puppy's crate with Crystal while he started with the first scheduled patients.

The puppy was named Eggnog for a while during the afternoon, and Freddy towards the evening. Becket had a continuing credits virtual class that he needed to complete before the end of the week to renew his license, so he reluctantly told Vivian that he'd be at her place after dinner, exchanging a long, sensuous kiss with her in the nurses station. "I probably won't be able to make it until tuck-in time," he said sadly. "There are some videos they won't let you skim through."

Vivian took the crate home with her when she left. "He'll have more fun at our house than cooped up in his crate, and we might as well accept that Tara has a puppy now."

"You're going to have to name him," Becket reminded her.

"Not Eggnog," Vivian said with a shudder.

"I liked Virtue," Crystal volunteered.

"That's a lot to live up to," Vivian said, pulling on her coat and gathering the puppy's crate into her arms with her purse. "See you tomorrow," she said to Crystal.

"See you…er, tonight," Becket said. They smiled foolishly at each other, but didn't kiss.

Crystal wasn't at all fooled, but she waited until Vivian left to say anything.

"You're really good for her."

"For Vivian?" It was ironic that Crystal would think that.

"She's a tough lady, and she'd never admit it, but she was grieving hard, and you've shown her that there's still life worth living."

And he was going to die and break her heart all over again.

"I think it's the other way around," he said honestly. "She's taught *me* how to live."

Crystal clutched her heart. "Oh my God, you're going to make me bawl. You guys are disgusting and perfect and worse than one of those sobbing books. Do you hear something? I have to go answer the phones now because someone is chopping onions in here. God, I hate menopause."

Becket smiled ruefully after her.

It was true, though. Vivian was an absolute inspiration. She had taken a terrible lot and found all the joy it was possible to find in it. She was an amazing mother, a sensuous lover, and a capable partner at the job. She was funny and full of life, worked harder than Becket had ever seen anyone work, and she loved with her whole heart. She unabashedly adored her children and her occupation and her town and…him.

She loved him.

Even knowing how short their time would be, she was all in. There were no doubts or reservations between them, no waiting for a better time, or delaying for any reason.

It was like they'd been made for each other, fitting together perfectly like nested spoons.

Fated.

Destined.

Mate, his unicorn sighed happily.

Becket had never been convinced of the concept of a mate. He only knew of it by wistful stories, the sources questionable. There was that one couple that a friend's cousin knew, and a lot of hopeful sighs from star-eyed girls and a few dreamy boys.

If she's my mate, why wouldn't fate give us more time together? he wondered, downloading his training video. A year didn't feel like nearly enough for the lifetime that he wanted to spend with her.

Who knows why fate does anything? his unicorn countered. *It's not like other people don't have tragic endings all the time. The only difference is that we know ours is coming.*

And that Becket could control it, but only in one direction, sliding it closer, but never further away. He knew that truth, and he had to accept this one, too.

She was his mate. She was his mate and he was entirely hers.

For all of the time that they had left.

Becket realized that he'd missed several vital minutes of the class video and cursed as he rewound it, wishing he could do the same with real time.

CHAPTER 31

Tara was up for the third time that evening.

"What is it, sweetheart?" Vivian asked in exasperation.

"I have to pee."

"Are you sure? Maybe you can just ignore it a little longer and fall asleep."

"I have to listen to my body," Tara protested, sidling for the bathroom.

Vivian sighed to hear her own words flung back at her. "Please hurry, darling. Don't use too much toilet paper."

Tara trotted for the bathroom and closed the door behind her—a sure sign that she was planning to dawdle as much as she could manage.

Vivian left the television paused in the middle of her grown-ups-only sitcom and scrolled through social media on her phone while she waited to tuck Tara back in.

"All done?" she prompted after a few moments of suspicious silence.

"Still going!" Tara sang back.

"Let's hurry!" Vivian tried again after she'd exhausted her Facebook feed and tired of memes.

"Wiping!"

Finally, Vivian heard Tara wash her hands with agonizing thoroughness and she emerged from the bathroom.

"Ready to be tucked back into bed?" Vivian said cheerfully, peeling the drowsing puppy from her lap and depositing him on the couch where she'd been sitting. He snuffled once in protest and fell back to sleep. "You need to get your sleep!"

"I'm not going to get any sleep," Tara said knowingly.

"Really?" Was this a challenge? Tara was usually the kind for subtle, boneless resistance, not outright disobedience. Vivian wasn't sorry to see her gaining confidence, but oh, it was frustrating how she chose to exercise it.

"You will, though." Tara didn't look exactly

like she was trying to argue. She looked thought-ful. A little distant, even. "You'll sleep."

"I'm going to sleep, but you aren't?" Vivian was tired, but she didn't think it was just her own exhaustion that was making this conversation make no sense. Was she trying to put too much faith in the sleepy ramblings of a four-year-old?

"They'll try to hurt us, but they won't," Tara said confidently.

All of Vivian's exhaustion vanished into alarm. "Who's going to try to hurt us, honey?"

"They *won't*," Tara said.

That was no comfort whatsoever.

"Who are you talking about? Are they people that we know?" Vivian prodded. Was this fore-sight or was Tara just trying to keep from going to bed? Sometimes she spoke with exactly the same confidence about things that never hap-pened as those that did.

"It's scary, Mommy." Tara's face was crum-pling in distress.

Vivian swept her up into her arms. "I've got you, Tara. You know I'll take care of you. It's going to be okay." She tried to tamp down her own panic. She didn't know what Tara was talking about, but it clearly frightened her.

"You're going to be asleep, Mommy!" Tara said, sobbing into her shoulder.

Vivian rocked her gently. "Maybe it's just a dream," she said with confidence she didn't feel. "Maybe it's just a dream. I've got you, baby girl. I've got you. You'll sleep and it'll all be fine in the morning."

Tara soaked up all the comfort that Vivian could give her, and she thought that the little girl might actually fall asleep on her shoulder, going limp and quiet.

Then, abruptly, Tara sat up in her arms and looked at the door. "They're here."

The doorbell rang like a knife blade through the living room and Vivian didn't need any kind of supernatural sense of her own to know that it wasn't Becket. As she stood, frozen, trying to decide if she could dash forward and get the deadbolt shot home, or if it would be better to try to stay silent and pretend she wasn't there, the puppy woke up and started baying in alarm.

The door burst open, shattering around the latch in a way that suggested the deadbolt would have been useless, and Vivian had one moment to appreciate that indeed, Becket's bad guys were wearing a whole lot of black leather, before one of them was leveling a gun at her.

Tara screamed like a train whistle and Vivian instinctively turned to protect her with her entire body as she made slow sense of the words being shouted.

Something pricked at her shoulder, a bite of pain followed by numbness and Vivian got halfway down the hallway to the bedrooms before she crashed into a wall and fell to her knees, clumsily rolling to avoid crushing Tara. She heard Shane wake up and wail.

"Find the man!"

"There are kids here, what the hell?"

"Dammit, who gave the invasion order? We don't have authorization for this!" It almost sounded like there were two different teams, both of them shouting orders.

"We're supposed to use them for leverage."

"Does the boss know about this?"

"Get the dog, it might be one of them!"

Vivian's body was dulled. She couldn't feel Tara in her arms, but she could hear her crying. She tried to speak, to find words of comfort, but failed, only able to barely move her mouth. The puppy had escaped the men trying to catch him and rushed to lick her face, but Vivian couldn't feel his tongue on her skin, only distantly knew that it was happening. Her efforts to tell him to stop were futile.

She saw boots, watched Tara, struggling, being lifted from her line of sight, and then she had no sight at all and could only fall asleep, exactly as the little girl had predicted.

CHAPTER 32

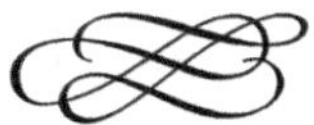

One of the problems with instinct is that it was sometimes just like panic, so strong and wild that Becket could not make sense of any of it or use its warning at all.

It was like that now, his unicorn plunging like it was being whipped and screaming in alarm.

Will you calm down? Becket begged. *I can't do anything with you freaking out in my head.*

Danger! Danger! Fear! Loss! Run! Danger! Terror!

Becket dredged down, deeper than his unicorn, using Vivian's example of epic patience to weather his unicorn's complete meltdown. He pulled the car that he was driving over to the shoulder, half up on the sidewalk, and put it in park before he could inadvertently cause an accident. Several other drivers swerved away and he was honked at.

CHILL, Becket roared, and he felt his unicorn pause in its panic. *If I kill us early running a red light, your little nervous breakdown won't have done any good at all. Now regroup and tell me what's happening!*

His unicorn shuddered and panted, but calmed. *Vivian,* it said achingly. *The children! Something is **wrong**.*

But it couldn't say *what.*

Becket put the car into drive and pulled recklessly back out into traffic, just clearing a hydrant and missing a bicyclist with flashing lights. More cars honked at him as he wove forward, full speed for Vivian's house.

Her lights were still on, bright behind the pulled curtains, and Becket thought for a blissful moment that everything was going to be fine and Vivian was going to laugh at him…then he saw that there was light around the latch of her front door.

He drove directly up onto her lawn so that he wouldn't have to walk any further than necessary, and was appalled to find that her door had been broken in and then imperfectly shut. The house itself was silent. The television had a sitcom paused on the screen, a woman brandishing a pumpkin frozen with her mouth open. Becket bolted for the back bedrooms. Tara's bed looked slept in, her blankets folded back like she'd just gotten up. Shane's crib was empty. His diaper bag was hanging by the door, but the car seat was gone.

The puppy's crate was vacant, the door open.

Gone! Wrong! Gone! Taken!

Becket didn't need instinct to know what had happened. It was his worst fear. His past had caught up with him and when Hunter hadn't been able to find him specifically, he had taken the dearest things to him.

Vivian, he thought achingly. Tara. Shane. The puppy that Vivian refused to name.

CHAPTER 33

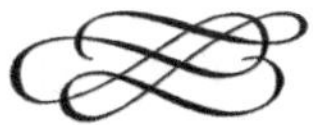

Vivian had a few flashes of consciousness that were hard to put together into sense. There was a long, prone journey, and she was dimly aware of Tara and Shane crying, of someone trying to comfort them, of helplessly struggling to regain her senses.

When she woke up the last time, she was lying in a bed, and a ceiling above her started to come into focus.

"Mama? Mommy?"

"She's going to be okay," a strange voice assured Tara. "Look, she's starting to wake up!"

"Mommy, there's a dolly! Hi, Mommy!"

An unfamiliar doll was inserted between Vivian's view of the ceiling and the end of her nose, and then dropped onto her face. "Oh, sowwy, Mommy! It's okay, Dolly!"

Vivian started to recognize her own limbs and tried to sit up, failing as Tara retrieved the doll from her face and tried to comfort her.

Someone helped her sit up and pressed a glass of water to her lips.

Her throat was painfully dry and sore.

A barbiturate? She felt a little dirty inside, like her body was trying to protest what had been done to it, but she didn't think she'd been hurt. It was hard to think sensibly at all.

"I apologize for the team's...enthusiasm," the strange man said kindly.

Once she could focus on him, she saw that he was middle-aged, with rather severe features. He was wearing a fine silk shirt and had the kind of haircut that had to be styled in a salon. He looked genuinely concerned for her. Tara, who was usually painfully shy and clingy around strangers, seemed to be perfectly comfortable with him and was trying to show him an unfamiliar fashion doll.

"The dose of the drug that you took was calibrated for a shifter's metabolism and it took longer than I had hoped for you to come around.

I want to assure you that we mean no harm to you or to your children."

"Shane? The puppy?" Vivian rasped. The abduction was coming back to her now, in flashes of memory.

"Goldilocks," Tara said firmly. "I'm going to call him Goldilocks."

"That's a girl's name," Vivian reminded her. To her relief, Tara seemed perfectly sound and happy.

"He can be a girl," she said with perfect four-year-old logic.

"The dog is fine," the man promised. "Your son is sleeping."

Vivian hated having to lean against this stranger who was clearly involved in their capture, even if she didn't recognize him from the invasion, but she obediently drank the water he pressed on her, knowing she would need it to clear the drugs from her system.

The stranger cautiously took the water glass away and let go and Vivian found that she could remain seated without him as he rose to put it on a desk nearby.

She looked around at the room, blinking to clear her vision.

They were in a plushly appointed room with two beds and an array of high tech medical equipment. Large windows framed in heavy curtains showed only a city-lit night sky, giving her no specific clue about where they might be. Shane was in a car seat on the floor, the puppy sleeping bonelessly next to him. There were couches and a desk. The tidy remains of a meal were spread out on the desk, as well as a metal pitcher beaded with condensation. There was quiet music playing, something classical on a tastefully invisible sound system.

Martha Stewart, but medical, she remembered Becket saying.

The other bed was occupied by a slight figure attached to an alarming array of machines that were blinking and whirring. Under the music, she recognized the sound of a ventilator, and the regular hiss of sequential compression sleeves. A muted EKG betrayed a sluggish heartbeat and an ICP monitor made Vivian suspect a brain injury.

It was an old man in a coma, Vivian decided, and not in good shape. She guessed that these people were hoping to have Becket heal this man and anger helped her burn off more of the lingering drugs in her system.

How dare they expect Becket to sacrifice what remained of his life to prolong the days of some entitled old man! She glanced at the stranger. Was this his son? Or just someone who had been paid well to ensure that the man lived a long, healthy life at the expense of Becket?

As if he guessed her train of thought, the man introduced himself. "My name is David Pincer."

When Vivian didn't volunteer her name in return, he gave it to her wryly. "You're Vivian Yang."

"You could just return us to our home now, since you know where it is," Vivian suggested. "I wouldn't press charges for the home invasion and drugging and kidnapping and endangering my children if you just let us all go."

David chuckled. "That's big of you, Ms. Yang. But I'm afraid that I can't do that until an exchange has been made."

"You're exchanging me? For what?" Vivian hoped that she looked innocent.

"Philip Singlehorn—I believe you know him as James Becket? He was our goal and I apologize again that you got mixed up in this. We had intelligence that he was at that address and my...associate...decided without consulting me to take you and your family as assurance of his cooperation."

Becket. Vivian's worst fear was confirmed. No, maybe not her worst fear. She'd been afraid that they would know about Tara and want to keep her for their own nefarious purposes. A fortune-telling child would be worth a lot to people who were willing to kidnap and blackmail an entire family and a helpless puppy.

"What do you want with him?" Vivian asked, heart in her throat. "I won't let you hurt him."

David gave her a raking look. "I'm not a monster, Vivian. I'm not going to put him in a lab or torture him. I just need his particular talents to help…someone close to me." His eyes flickered the slightest bit towards the medical bed.

"Mommy, I'm hungry."

"She wouldn't eat while you were asleep, but there's food," David said. Maybe Vivian's cautions about taking food from strangers had stuck, even if Tara had accepted the doll as obvious bribery for good behavior. "Whatever you want, name it. I'll call it in downstairs."

Vivian's stomach threatened to rebel but Tara looked up at him hopefully. "Candy?" she suggested.

"Chicken tenders?" Vivian countered with something she knew Tara would eat. "And a glass of milk." The last thing she needed to do was sugar up Tara on the heels of her traumatic journey. She was furious that these people, whoever they were, were subjecting her children to this kind of stress, and she had a wicked headache blooming at the bridge of her nose where the doll had hit her. She knew that she sounded short and ungrateful and wasn't even slightly sorry for it.

David went to the big double doors and Vivian recognized an opportunity. If she could somehow get her children—and the sleeping puppy—to the window, maybe she could get them out and...scale down the building? She quickly accepted the futility of the plan, particularly since she couldn't even muster the strength to stand yet, and she observed that there were armed guards at the doors who greeted David and spoke quietly with him. Then David was shutting the doors and walking back towards them.

"It should be here in about twenty minutes," he said.

"Thank you," Vivian said automatically and Tara echoed her cheerfully, marching the doll along the edge of the bed.

David went to the other bed and Vivian caught the agonized look on his face. This wasn't a paid position for him, it was deeply personal. Which meant it was going to be even harder to get out of. She abandoned her fleeting idea of begging for mercy or offering her life savings for their freedom.

She swung her legs to the side of the bed and David made no move to stop her, settling instead in a chair by the man's bed. Tara raised her arms for a hug and Vivian gathered the girl up into her lap to hold her tight and soak up comfort from her safety.

She had been on top of a quilt with a light throw over her legs. Whatever else was happening, there didn't seem to be any intention of keeping them uncomfortable.

She bent over, hampered by Tara, to confirm that Shane was indeed slumbering peacefully. The puppy woke up enough to thump his tail a few times in greeting and was unconscious again. Vivian remembered him whining through most of the haze of her drugged travel; he must have worn himself out on the trip.

They hadn't grabbed Shane's diaper bag during the abduction, but someone had given some thought to their needs. There was a small box of diapers in his size, if not his preferred brand, an unopened package of wipes, a bottle and three kinds of formula, some gourmet baby food, several toys besides the doll that was being disrobed now, and a dozen folded blankets and bibs. There were even a few cans of puppy food and two dishes, one of them filled with water, as well as a box of puppy pads.

Vivian wondered wryly if she would get to keep them at the end of their ordeal as some kind of consolation prize, then remembered what the end of their ordeal would entail and had a stab of cold fear.

Where was Becket? Was he safe? Would instinct warn him away from following them? The idea of being bait for a trap for him made Vivian's already unsettled stomach seize in fear.

Tara wriggled free of her embrace, more interested in her new prize than Vivian's hugs. "I'll name her Goldilocks!" she declared, removing more of the doll's clothing. Vivian refrained from pointing out that the doll's hair was dark. Maybe it didn't matter.

"That's a pretty name, sweetheart."

Although David was by appearances reading a tablet, Vivian was keenly aware of his watchful glances and she cursed her sluggish mind for not providing any kind of solution or escape plan.

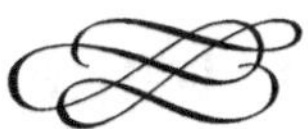

CHAPTER 34

Becket sat in Vivian's empty house for a long while, breathing in the silence.

Then he dug into his pocket and stared at his phone as if he expected it to ring.

Hunter wouldn't be after him merely for revenge. This took *resources*. Which meant that someone was paying for him. Some hopeless case that only he had any chance of curing, for a client with deep pockets. Hunter wouldn't be working for pennies. Maybe he had a whole hospital of desperate people lined up.

I hurt them once, his unicorn snarled. *I could hurt them again.*

Becket thought that it was ironic that his unicorn, supposedly a creature of peace and healing, was the one who was so bloodthirsty.

Their previous escape from Hunter had been a grisly show of force. Becket wasn't sure if any of his men had died, but he knew that he'd wounded them grievously in the battle, not shy about using hooves or horn. When he finally realized that Hunter was only using him, didn't believe the price that he was paying, and had no intention of releasing his services, he'd snapped.

Hunter had been ready for his escape attempt, but he hadn't been ready for Becket's ferocity.

Becket wasn't proud that he'd lost control, but he wasn't sorry, either.

His story to Vivian was vague about the details, only saying that he'd left Hunter's service. He hadn't wanted to admit how angry he was, or how vicious he'd been with Hunter's men, but when he closed his eyes, he could still see it, and he could still remember how it had felt to trample flesh.

They lied and tried to trap us, his unicorn growled. *They deserved no mercy.*

You are a dichotomous creature, Becket observed.

No more than you are, it countered. *Healing is the same coin as hurting, just the other side of it.*

Most of their battle for freedom had been physical, but when Becket was sure that they would lose to the superior numbers and might of Hunter's men, he had unleashed a dark version of his healing power, sending them to their knees with searing pain.

It had cost him dearly in days to live, but won their escape in a terrible, final way and Becket had sworn to never use his power that way again.

That was why he thought that Hunter hadn't pursued him.

He was afraid of Becket.

And now, something must have happened, to overcome that fear.

Money, Becket thought. With Hunter it was always money, and the power that came with it. Did he have some method of curtailing Becket's power now? Had he come to believe Becket's story of spending his actual life when he used his magic? Or did he think that having Vivian and her children as hostages would secure his cooperation?

Because it would, Becket knew.

He would do anything for Vivian, for Tara's big mournful eyes, for Shane's slobbery grins. He would give the last of his life to save them.

He had no way to contact Hunter; that information had been lost with everything else he'd left behind.

But he knew that Hunter's men would be back soon enough, sent back to watch for him.

And he'd be ready to go with them.

CHAPTER 35

The puppy roused enough to stagger to the desk with them when the chicken tenders were delivered, ate one, and then flopped onto his side to sleep again.

Tara consumed her food as slowly as was humanly possible, challenging Vivian's understanding of that limit once again. The milk was served in a heavy pint glass and when Tara reached two greasy hands for it, Vivian wisely intercepted her and held it while Tara sipped, much as David had done with the water for her. There was a small pile of candy on the tray as well, and a bowl of gourmet corn chips that Vivian took a few of, hoping to settle her stomach.

Some of Tara's slowness was clearly exhaustion. Vivian coaxed as many tenders into her as she could manage.

"She can sleep in the far bed," David said kindly, when Tara's head started to bob.

He'd been quiet through their prolonged meal, though Vivian was keenly aware of his presence in the room. She didn't particularly want to acknowledge him.

She definitely didn't want to pity him.

Vivian finished the milk and forced herself to eat one of the chicken pieces as Tara stubbornly chewed on her last tired bite and protested her creeping sleep. Vivian knew that she would need food in her stomach herself to shake off the last of the drugs that were still making her limbs feel like dead weights, and she thought that the chicken would probably have tasted good if her digestive system wasn't still in rebellion.

There was an accessible bathroom right off the room and if Tara had eaten slowly, she went to the bathroom even more slowly, insisting on Vivian's presence for the process even if she was no longer at the point where she needed help. One down on the potty training, two to go, Vivian thought wryly, thinking of Shane and the puppy.

She hoped he peed on the fancy carpet during the night.

The puppy had followed them to the bathroom, camping out in front of the door while Vivian washed Tara's face off and had her swish some water in her mouth to make up for not being able to brush her teeth.

He stood up as they came out and followed them closely to the bed, whining when Tara climbed up without him.

Vivian exchanged a defiant look with David and lifted the puppy up onto the bed with Tara, to her sleepy delight. She pulled the throw over Tara and the puppy rotated a few times and then fell over on his side in the cup of Tara's body.

They were both asleep in moments.

Vivian was heartily tempted to join them, but instead, she drew the privacy curtain around them.

In a perfectly predictable pattern, Shane woke up and gave a whimper of protest.

Vivian rocked the car seat and after a blurble and a few tired waves of his hands, Shane went back to sleep. She crouched next to him for a moment, stroking back his fuzzy hair. He was probably due for his first haircut soon. He'd lost all of the hair he was born with, but it had finally grown back, dark and thick.

When he was quiet and unconscious again, she stood and went to face David.

There was an old-fashioned chart hanging at the end of the hospital bed and Vivian picked it up without asking permission—he had, after all, kidnapped her and she felt like certain liberties in return were not unreasonable.

"Is this your father?" she asked.

What she could see of the face around the medical mask was wizened, with thin, white hair dusting his scalp. The arms that lay on the blanket, attached to IVs and sensors, were frail and thin, and covered with leathery, weathered skin.

"This is my son," David said, and Vivian gazed in shock at the statistics on the chart as the pieces fell into place.

"He has progeria," she said.

"You're a doctor?" David said suspiciously.

"I'm a nurse," Vivian said without any of the shame that some people attached to a lesser title. "And I'm a damn good one. I did a great deal of my residency in a clinic that did research on obscure childhood disease. Progeria was one of the ones that we were collecting data on. There is no cure."

"There is no *medical* cure," David corrected her. "But Phillip—Becket—could heal him."

And treating him would probably kill Becket.

Vivian's head was still pounding, making it hard to think. She didn't think David knew about the catch to Becket's power. To him, it was a simple equation and he was willing to spend his money and flex his power in order to make it happen.

"The average survival age of progeria is only fourteen," she said. Timothy was already pushing those averages at sixteen, and he looked like a dwarven eighty years old.

"Timothy is a fighter," David said fiercely. "I won't give up on him."

Vivian gave David an appraising look. He was a powerful man, and he clearly had money and connections and brains. And he loved his child, the way that Vivian loved hers. It wasn't that he was cruel, only that he was desperate.

"His heart is giving out," she said, glancing over his chart.

"He's in a chemical coma until we can get a heart transplant."

There was no legitimate medical service that would put a healthy donor heart in a vessel so fragile and doomed.

But then, this was definitely not a legitimate medical service.

"What do you know about Becket? Philip. Becket." Vivian asked cautiously. Philip sounded all wrong for him, if not quite as wrong as Sparkle Lightfoot.

"He's a unicorn," David said matter-of-factly. "A literal unicorn shifter who can heal miraculously."

"You know about shifters." It felt weird and unnatural to talk about them out loud. Vivian wrestled with how much to trust him with. She'd spent so much time keeping it a secret that it felt like there was a great weight on her tongue.

"I know enough," David said dismissively. "They live in the shadows of our society."

"No," Vivian said gently. "They live beside you in sunlight. Your neighbors and cashiers and teachers and plumbers." If she could humanize Becket, and other shifters, maybe she could win sympathy in David's heart. It was clear that he had feelings, the way he was grieving for his son. She just had to show him that those feelings applied to others. "They are not unnatural or evil. They are people. They are parents and children."

David didn't look like he felt particularly

charitable about a secret society of animal-shifting citizens.

"Becket's gifts come with a cost," Vivian said, hoping the truth would be enough. "Every time that he heals someone, his own life becomes shorter."

That did earn her a sharp, thoughtful look and Vivian tried not to draw too much hope from it.

"He's used it enough that he only has about a year left to live at all," Vivian said, then wondered if she should have admitted it. Maybe David would argue that Becket was already doomed and use it as justification for destroying him.

"Are you a shifter?" he asked, point blank.

Vivian hesitated, then shook her head. "I'm not."

David's eyes narrowed. "But your husband was?" He looked swiftly towards the curtained bed where Tara slept. "Your children are." It wasn't a question.

Vivian tamped down her desire to stand and put her body uselessly to block his line of sight. If she trusted him to be the bigger man, maybe he would be. She had to be patient and brave, and make it clear that this was not a victimless crime.

She didn't confirm his guess, but she didn't deny it. "Shifters aren't the bad guys here," she said pointedly. "They aren't kidnapping people and terrifying their children." Not that Tara seemed particularly terrified. Vivian remembered that Tara could see the future and wondered if she should be comforted by the little girl's serenity. Surely, if something awful was actually going to happen, Tara would be more upset by it?

Did David look uncomfortable at her reminder that they'd been abducted and brought here as hostages? "I don't even know if Becket can cure this," Vivian pressed. "Progeria is a genetic mutation. Correcting something like that is a lot different than closing up an open wound or even burning out an infection. If we can't fix it medically, why would you believe that it can be fixed magically?"

David's gaze was unwavering. "Because I *have* to believe it," he said simply.

Vivian felt well enough to eat the rest of Tara's food, leaving aside the rich candy. She knew that whatever happened next, she needed her wits and her strength. She brought the plate to sit across from David defiantly.

I'm a person, she wanted him to see. *A real person with a family of my own, and you can't simplify me into a pawn in your equation to save your son.*

She asked him about Timothy's progression, and after a few halting starts, David told her stories of the boy's childhood, hobbled by the disability, his fight against his failing body, his unending cheer in the face of adversity.

"He's such a fighter," David said tenderly. "It isn't fair that this is his end."

Don't talk to me about fair, Vivian wanted to spit. "He sounds like a good kid," she only said mildly.

"What is it like having a shifter child?" David wanted to know. "Is she super-powered? Can *she* heal?"

Vivian knew that she was not a particularly good liar, but she considered her words with care. "Tara is a unicorn," she said cautiously. "But not like Becket. She is a kirin and her…powers… are rather different, and not developed yet."

She wondered as she spoke if she'd made a grave error of judgment. Was it naive of her to think that there was a good person in David, and that she could influence his next actions by appealing to his better nature by being honest and kind? Was his glance towards the bed where Tara was sleeping slightly speculative?

She steered the conversation to sweet stories about Tara and Shane, about raising kids and juggling a career after Jin's death. She was frank about her loss, and David *seemed* sympathetic.

And she couldn't tell stories about them without bringing Becket into the narrative. "I don't know how I got along without him," she said frankly. "He's so good with the kids. The clinic is lucky to have him as a doctor there. *I'm* lucky to have him. Even for just a little while."

David's phone rang and he rose to walk to the far end of the spacious room.

Vivian strained to listen while pretending she wasn't, but could make out nothing of the conversation.

She didn't have to wonder for long.

"They've got Becket," David said, walking back over the silent carpet to her. "He's on his way."

Vivian felt her chest seize in dismay, even as the idea of seeing Becket again filled her with conflicted joy.

CHAPTER 36

Becket didn't have to wait long in Vivian's house for them to return and find him. He was just starting to wonder if the police would be called first because of his car on the front lawn when he heard them scrabbling at the front door, and then around at the back door and under one of the windows.

Did they think he would try to get away?

"You don't have to lurk around," he scoffed out loud. "I know what you're here for, and I'm prepared to make a trade. You don't hurt them, and I'll go quietly."

As he'd promised Vivian, they were dressed dramatically in black leather, and terribly out of place in Vivian's quiet neighborhood. He was surprised that the neighborhood watch hadn't already been called.

There were a half dozen of them, and they were better armed than Hunter's guards had been in the past. Maybe he was becoming more paranoid. Or maybe he remembered how much damage Becket had been able to do when they parted.

One of the men had a dart gun. "You don't need to bother," Becket told him, eyeing the weapon. "I'll go willingly. You already have what I want."

The goons exchanged looks and one of them stepped outside to make a swift call, returning to gesture for Becket to come with them.

There was a van out front, and it drove them to an airstrip out of Bozeman.

No one bothered with conversation.

The private flight from Bozeman to Denver was only a couple of hours, but they sat on the private runway waiting for clearance until Becket's bruising handler was agitated and spent some time on the phone apologizing to Hunter. Becket tried not to fidget or worry for Vivian. He was curious to observe that the men were of two very different classes, some of them rough and some of them considerably more poised and well-spoken.

Becket didn't give them any trouble as they finally disembarked the plane. He briefly considered trying to get the attention of airfield security… even if he couldn't actually get away, he could throw up enough of a fuss to put Hunter and his hired men under uncomfortable public scrutiny.

What he really wanted to do was shift into his unicorn form and skewer Hunter straight through the chest when he saw him at the bottom of the airline stairs. Was it worth a little life to make this man suffer?

But he still didn't know for sure where Vivian and her kids were, and he wasn't willing to risk their mistreatment.

"Hunter," he said with cold courtesy as they met. It was windbreaker weather and he wished he could control the goosebumps rising on his bare arms.

"*Philip*," Hunter said, his voice silky and low. "Thank you for making this a more civilized transaction."

"It's just business," Becket said with a shrug, remembering how often Hunter had said those words.

"We've got a car so you won't have to trot," Hunter said jovially. "Blindfold him."

The ride into Denver was a dark and jostling journey, and Becket felt the chilly outside air give way to a warmer interior.

There was a long elevator ride—the building probably had an amazing view—and then he was being roughly led into a room with soft acoustics.

"Becket!" Vivian's voice was quiet and urgent and when his blindfold was removed and his eyes finally adjusted, Becket thought that he'd never seen anything so beautiful. There were tears in her blue eyes but her jaw was set and she looked unharmed.

"They said they wouldn't hurt you," Becket said. He stepped away from his guards and one of them grabbed him roughly by the arm.

"Leave him be!" Vivian snapped, stepping forward just as Becket twisted out of his grasp. "I'm not hurt!" she assured him.

"Just abducted with your children," Becket said. "Is Tara...?"

"Tara and Shane are sleeping." Vivian glanced behind her towards a curtained bed. "They're fine, too."

For now.

"This is David," Vivian introduced, like she

was the power in the room. Somehow, that didn't surprise him. She was fearless and fierce, and of course she'd have everything under control. "His son has advanced progeria. He's in the late stages of multiple organ failure and is being kept in a medical coma, for now." Trust her to have already diagnosed the case and have all the details he needed. She was everything he had ever wanted in a helpmate and a partner.

David stepped forward to shake his hand, like this was just a simple business transaction and no one had been kidnapped at all. "A pleasure to meet you," he said, without a hint of remorse.

One of Hunter's thuggish guards stepped forward and slapped down Becket's hand before he could shake with it. David did look affronted by that, like he was expecting everything to be more civilized. He seemed like a different class of man than Hunter. Rich, yes, and powerful, in that soft way of someone who had never had to work for anything in his life. Hunter always looked like he was expecting a betrayal.

Maybe because he was the kind of person who betrayed others.

"I'll need my hands free to do the work you want," Becket said, when one of the goons offered to zip-tie him. It wasn't entirely true, but Becket gambled that none of them really knew how he did what he did.

"Leave him free," Hunter agreed grudgingly. "But if he tries to escape, shoot him. No, shoot the woman."

"Shoot the woman?" Vivian snarled.

Becket gave a dry chuckle. "Why don't you just threaten to shoot the children, Hunter? Let everyone here see what a low snake of a human being you actually are. Hiding behind hostages? Getting your men to do your dirty work as part of your grasp for power? How much is David paying you guys, anyway? Enough for your actual *souls?*"

"Shooting a woman wasn't part of our arrangement," David said disapprovingly. "Children weren't part of the agreement at all."

"I'm standing right here, you know," Vivian snapped. "And those are my children."

"No one will hurt them," David promised, eyeing Hunter for agreement.

Hunter didn't acknowledge the look or the promise. "Get to work, Becket. The sooner you do this, the sooner we're done here."

Hunter didn't relish this relationship any more than Becket did, he realized. He was still afraid of Becket's power, and that gave Becket an advantage, however slim.

As he was trying to figure out how to use that advantage, Hunter prodded him over to the bed. "The deal is simple. You save his life, I get paid, everyone goes home in one piece."

"It's not that easy," Vivian protested.

"It's a very straight-forward trade."

"You don't understand," Vivian said desperately. "What you're asking him to do will kill him!"

"Is that what he told you?" Hunter scoffed.

"Is it true?" David asked.

It was to David that Vivian turned. "I know that you care a great deal for your son, but I don't believe that you would trade a man's life for his. Becket's gift has a terrible cost on him. Whatever Hunter has told you, you aren't asking him to simply perform an expensive surgery or wave a magical wand, you're asking him to give up the last of his *own* life to save your son. I don't think that you understood that price, and I trust that you won't force him to pay it."

Becket wanted to protest that the equation wasn't actually that simple. It was a boy's chance at an entire life for a year of his own. His *last* year, to be true, but he already knew too well that was galloping down on him, as inevitable as a sunset.

He also wanted to warn Vivian not to put her trust in the goodness of David. His experience with people was that they were short-sighted and full of greed more than they weren't. Surely Vivian's pleas would fall on deaf ears. And it was hard to blame David. The love of a father for his child was a powerful force and desperate people did desperate things. If he'd been in David's situation and given a chance to save Tara, was there anything he wouldn't do? He'd certainly have spent his last magic without a single second thought if that had been Tara in that bed facing a terrible end too soon.

"Vivian..." he cautioned, but he wasn't sure what argument he would make.

"Can you save my son?" David wanted to know. "*Can* you?"

Becket closed his eyes and felt his unicorn probe at the future. It was always a curious sensation, like poking a fork into half-cooked meat. Was it done? Could you tell by the resistance to the tines? It was never as precise as a thermal probe.

We can save him, his unicorn said confidently. *It's a flaw, **here**, that we can fix.*

It was sometimes disorienting when his unicorn showed him things, because they didn't line up with the pictures in scientific texts. DNA wasn't the tidy twisted strand of color-coded nucleotides, it was a rush of colors and temperatures, ordered by harmony.

His unicorn could see the thread of discord, could see exactly where to pluck to unwind the wrongness in his genetic makeup that had caused Timothy's malady. And it would cost everything they had left. His own end would be *now*, not some romantic *someday*, not comfortably far off. There would be no time left for the rest of the *Becket* list.

Can we undo the damage, or would it only prevent more degradation? Becket persisted. The boy was already so far gone.

But his unicorn was sure. They could turn back the injury, heal the skin, revitalize the degradation of the flesh. It was possible to give Timothy not only his life, but his youth back. He might never grow as tall as he otherwise could have, but he would have health and strength again.

They could do it.

But should they?

CHAPTER 37

*V*ivian held her breath, half-hoping that Becket would lie. All he had to do was say that Timothy's death was inevitable and surely David would see the sense in letting them all go. If there was nothing that could be done, what could you do but grieve…and value the time that you had left?

But Becket's eyes opened and he looked at David with sympathy and unnerving acceptance. "I can save him. It will take everything I have left."

"No!" Vivian protested. "You can't do that!"

Support came from an utterly unexpected quarter. "No, you can't," Hunter said, his lips thin and grim.

Vivian thought for a beautiful moment that

David was going to prove a better man than his supervillain name had indicated that he might be, that he would agree that Becket's life was not a fair trade for his son's health. She was hopeful that he would relinquish his claim on Becket's services altogether.

Then, Hunter, in a fit of humanity, would let them go, and maybe she could recommend David to her therapist for some solid grief counseling. It wasn't a perfect ending, because she would still have to wrestle with losing Becket herself in far too short a time, but it was the best one that Vivian could see.

But Hunter was not protesting that Becket should not make a sacrifice of his life. He believed Becket at last, because Vivian did. But that wasn't making him choose to release Becket.

Quite the opposite.

He had his gun leveled at Becket and Vivian sucked in her breath as he seemed to reconsider his aim. The muzzle swung to face her.

It wasn't that Vivian was particularly frightened of guns. She'd grown up in Montana and shot her share of tin cans off of fence rails with rifles on hot August afternoons.

But there was something visceral about having a handgun pointed at her heart, knowing that this man wouldn't hesitate to pull the trigger if it got him what he wanted.

And he wanted Becket for himself.

She chilled to her toes in absolute terror and wasn't sure how much of it was for herself and how much was for the man she loved.

"This is an unfortunate wrinkle," Hunter said coldly. "I had planned to wring more than one of these out of you and now I'm forced to improvise for the highest bidder, which, I'm sorry to inform you, Mr. Pincer, is not you."

"You're backing out of our deal?" David said dangerously.

Vivian knew that she was expendable in this negotiation, and she was painfully aware of Tara behind her, sleeping with the puppy behind the curtain, Shane in the car seat nearby. Of all the possible losses she faced now, she could not bear the idea of leaving them unprotected.

"There's no reason to be hasty," she said, hating how thin and terrified her voice sounded.

She focused on saving her pride, because it was an abstract thing that did not have terrible consequences if she failed.

"Listen up!" she said more firmly, setting her hands at her hips. "None of you have authority to speak for another man's life and you are sadly mistaken if you think I'm going to let you cow me into acting the victim so that you can force Becket to make a martyr out of himself. Put that gun down, right now!" She said it like she was telling Tara not to run out into traffic: firm, frantic, and final.

For the space of one breath, Vivian thought that her desperate bluff was going to work.

But Hunter only smiled at her. "A gunshot wound will be significantly simpler to heal than a genetic deficiency," he observed. "That should leave plenty of Becket's life source for the rest of what I need."

And then he pulled the trigger.

"No!" Becket's shout was loud enough to wake the dead and at the same time, David yelped, "You can't!" Both of them dived for Hunter, too late.

Even as Vivian braced herself for the pain and impact of being shot, Hunter's gun jammed.

Behind her, Tara shrieked in fear and the puppy woke along with her and began to bark in confusion and alarm.

Hunter was looking quizzically at his gun as Becket got to him, and his guards started to move forward protectively but David roared an order that froze them all. "None of you are to hurt him! I'll see you never work in this business again if you lay one finger on Philip Singlehorn!"

Despite Becket's ridiculous name, David's words had considerably more weight than Vivian's had and the goons stopped in their steps, uncertain.

"No one will ever follow him again!" Tara cried, scrambling out from behind the curtain and throwing herself at Vivian.

As Vivian caught Tara, Becket's fist connected with Hunter's jaw and the gun went flying across the room, thumping onto the thick carpet.

David only let him get in one additional blow before he ordered the guards to break up the fight, and they obeyed him to a man. Was it because they recognized his superior power or financial clout? Was it because Hunter had asked them to shoot an unarmed woman and done so himself when they wouldn't? Had David had control over them the entire time? Was Tara speaking the future or had she *controlled* it in some way? Vivian was not sure she had ever witnessed such a total and utter change of loyalties in so short a time and she recognized that she was fixating on that because she still wasn't sure why she was still alive.

"Get him out of here," David snarled. "My

men will show you where to put him." The guards frog-marched a spitting Hunter from the room and shut the doors behind them, leaving only two who were clearly David's personal guards behind.

Becket let them take Hunter and closed the distance to Vivian to gather her up in his arms. She felt rather than heard his sob of relief as her face crushed into his chest. Maybe it was her own sob of relief.

Tara was sobbing even louder, wrapping her arms around Vivian with strength disproportionate to her size.

The puppy was not sobbing at all, only romping and yipping and trying to figure out how to coax them to play with him now that he was awake and ready to frolic and whyyyyy wasn't anyone paying attention to him?

"You're okay!" Becket whispered. "You're okay!"

"He was going to shoot me," Vivian said into his chest, before she could worry that Tara would hear. "He did shoot me. The gun jammed."

"It was lucky," Becket said fiercely.

"I'm lucky!" Tara wailed. "I'm *lucky!*"

"This is very touching," David said, and Vivian felt a chill through her shocky flush. David's son was still dying and Becket was the only one who could save him. David could yet force him to do it.

But he wasn't looking at Becket, he was looking at Tara. "You're a unicorn, too," he said thoughtfully.

Panic flooded Vivian. She had made a terrible mistake confiding in David and now she would pay the ultimate price. "Not that kind of unicorn!" she protested. "She's a kirin, a Chinese unicorn. She can't heal like Becket can. She's not worth anything to you!"

"I'm lucky!" Tara repeated through her tears.

Vivian could feel Becket's tension in every inch of his body. It felt like he'd turned to stone against her, every muscle ready to protect Tara from David with his life if that's what it came to.

And that's what it had come to.

"I'll heal him," he said to David as he drew back from Vivian. "Let them go, promise me that you'll never bother them again, take them back to their lives and I'll give you my life to save his."

CHAPTER 38

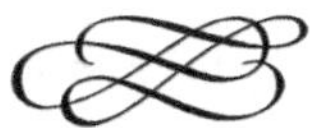

$\mathcal{B}$ecket watched David wrestle with his offer. A life for a life, freely offered, for the freedom of the family that Becket loved like his own.

And finally the man shook his head, wearily, and his shoulders slumped in defeat.

"I wouldn't hurt them. I'm ashamed that you think I might, even if Tara did have your gifts. When I dealt with Hunter, I swear that I didn't know what it might cost you. I didn't know that Vivian and Tara and Shane would get swept up in this." David looked down at the retriever puppy, who had given up trying to get Vivian and Tara to play and was begging at his feet for affection. He crouched and petted the puppy's head and ears, precipitating a wiggling, whining collapse of pure, innocent ecstasy. "I didn't think about who else might get caught up in this at all."

It was hard to think evil of a sad man petting a joyful puppy and Becket tried not to let hope loose in his heart.

"I'll send them all back to their lives and give them the protection that I can. I can't ask you to save Timothy, and I won't. I will take a lesson from you both and treasure what time we have left." David stood, to the puppy's disappointment, and went to the hospital bed where his son lay.

Becket looked at David as he sank down to sit on the bed, his head bent over his dying son in defeat and acceptance, saying final words of love and support.

Then Becket looked back at Vivian, who was watching him with suspicion in her eyes.

He wasn't being forced into anything.

David would let them go and Becket could hoard his healing power. He might have a year together with Vivian, maybe even more. They would enjoy a brief calendar of holidays and happiness as he helped her raise her children…and then said goodbye to them. Shane might remember him, Tara would probably consider him a father figure, Becket's memories fresher than her own father's.

He could almost not fathom the amount of joy they might share, the nights tucking the kids in, romping with the puppy who would inevitably have a name by then, making cookies together in Vivian's cozy kitchen. He imagined staying at the clinic with her full time, not just for a few months, working side-by-side...

...and never able to use his healing power.

He knew firsthand how hard it would be to never use his abilities, knowing that his end was pounding down on them *anyway*. He would have to fight against the regret and selfishness he would feel, always faced with what he could do and what he *might* have done.

Or, he could treasure the brief time that he'd had with Vivian as part of her little family, and do what he was able with the gift he'd been given.

In the end, it was an easy choice. He only regretted the pain he would leave behind.

Vivian was still staring at him in horror, tears welling in her eyes. "Becket?" she said, because she had already guessed what he would do. "Becket?!"

It was easier to heal when he was in his unicorn shape, so Becket bowed his head and shifted, shimmering into a dappled white shape. He knew that it would take every scrap of magic that he had left to save Timothy and holding his human form while he did it could be a fatal distraction at a key moment.

"Oh!" Tara said in awe as he lifted one hoof at a time, settling into his equine body. "Pretty!"

Becket wanted to reassure her that her own unicorn form was just as pretty, but he couldn't speak like this.

David was staring at him. "I wasn't sure if I really believed it," he said. Was it hope in his voice?

"Becket! Don't you dare!"

"I couldn't even ask you to," David said, gazing up at him. Timothy's leathery hand was in his. "Not now that I know what it costs."

Becket drew in a breath of cleaning chemicals and iodine under the potpourri and leather and blew it out before he swung his head to Vivian, who stood up with Tara clinging to her legs. He desperately wanted her to understand, to get her forgiveness for what he was about to do.

"Can I touch him?" Tara begged.

Becket closed the distance between them and leaned down to snuffle in her hair and let the little girl touch his whiskered nose and gleaming horn. The puppy came cautiously forward to sniff his hooves and dance back when Becket took a step. The retriever fell onto his elbows in an invitation to play and Becket blew at him and danced away.

Tara joined the play and for a golden moment, all that mattered was the laughter of a child and the joyful whine of the puppy. Becket let them catch him and then left them wrestling together to step carefully to where Vivian still stood, with tears rolling down her cheeks.

She knew what he was going to do.

And she wasn't going to stop him.

Becket crowded in close and got his head over her shoulder so that he could pull her into a close cuddle. Vivian's arms crept up around his neck and he could feel her breath in his mane. For a long moment, they stood like that, drawing comfort from each other.

Finally, he drew reluctantly out of Vivian's embrace. "Oh, Becket," she said achingly. "You really are a unicorn."

Tara pulled the puppy out of his way, sobering. The puppy, oblivious, chewed gently on her hand and rolled over in her lap, his tail wagging happily as he squirmed. Tara looked anxiously at Vivian, then back at Becket.

David stood helplessly aside. Becket strode to the boy's side, his hooves silent in the carpet, and lowered his horn.

"You…don't have to," David said, but it was too late.

Becket poured his unicorn's magic down into the dying boy, vaguely aware that Vivian had gone around to the far side of his bed and was checking his vitals.

Fixing the genetic source was the hardest part, gently correcting the code in every cell of the boy. Then there was repairing the failing heart, strengthening the brittle bones, restoring the stressed organs, and refreshing the stretched skin. He didn't bother to regrow the hair, but the follicles became functional again; Timothy would grow it himself because he now had a lifetime of health ahead of him.

"He's stable," Vivian said, puncturing his trance. "You can stop," she begged.

"Timothy!" David cried. "He's breathing!"

Becket continued to heal the boy, paying careful attention to making his lungs strong and clearing his encrusted vascular system.

"Becket, you're done, you're done," Vivian told him desperately. "You did it, stop now!"

But Becket was too deep now, he was too committed to stop, and the magic flowed through him without resistance until it was completely extinguished. He lifted his impossibly heavy head and felt his unicorn form shed from him with the last of his power as he collapsed onto the bed next to the boy.

"He's not waking up," David said anxiously. "Should he be waking up?"

"His coma was drug-induced," Vivian said as she bolted around the bed and shoved David out of her way to gather Becket up in her arms. "He'll wake up when they are out of his system. Becket, Becket, what have you done? Why didn't you stop *sooner?*"

"I didn't want to bring you any grief," Becket said, feeling his unicorn's hoofbeats slow with the beating of his failing heart. "I wanted to spare you this."

"I know how to handle grief," Vivian said through clenched teeth. "I'm good with that. But I'm really bad with stupid, pointless self-sacrifice and I am going to be furious with you until the end of time." Her wrath felt palpable in the air between them, like a breath of fresh air in a stuffy room. It felt alive, but Becket knew that anger was not enough to keep him there.

"I love you," he said quietly, and he let go of the last of his life like a leaf in autumn…and fell.

CHAPTER 39

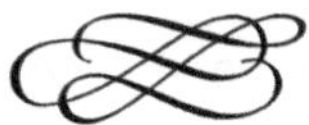

The chaos had woken Shane and he was wailing from his car seat, Tara was sobbing and trying to climb up on Vivian, the puppy was whining and probably peeing on something, the machines were still alarming, and Becket was dead.

Vivian felt like she was a shell of herself, fragile and fractured. She'd dared to fall in love with this man and he had the gall to *die* on her.

Then she remembered exactly how strong an eggshell could be, and she shook herself and looked around through the haze of her tears. He might have given up, but she *hadn't*.

They were in a fully-stocked hospice room and Vivian was a nurse who had done her time in the ER. She'd never brought anyone back from actual death, but she'd seen it happen, and here she was, in a recovery room, with a crash cart in the corner like a stroke of luck.

Tara was lucky.

She had to move fast, because luck was only worth so much, so she shot to her feet, pushing Tara away from her as she dumped Becket unceremoniously onto the bed. "I need you to stay back, honey. You, David, if you want to save your soul from putting us in this position in the first place, help me get him flat."

It was her emergency room voice, her get-out-of-my-way or get-in-line voice, and David leapt to obey her, grabbing Becket under the arms and helping her haul him up onto the second bed with strength of will, if not the strength of a shifter. Becket was denser than he looked, and it took precious seconds to get him straightened.

The crash cart was fully charged, another minor miracle of fortune, and there was a prepped injection of epinephrine that Vivian wrenched the cap off of. David, who had apparently seen enough medical television, had already ripped Becket's shirt open and Vivian lamented that she couldn't properly enjoy the beefcake portion of this show as she used her fingers to find the proper ribs and stabbed the needle directly down into his heart.

It took all her will to inject it slowly, and then she yanked it out and flung it down on the cart, reaching for the defibrillator paddles. "Clear!" she cried. "Tara, stay back, honey!" She ripped the pad covers off and slapped the paddles onto Becket's beautiful chest.

She thumbed the switch and it zapped like an industrial bug trap.

Vivian had a moment of hope as Becket's limbs twitched. She looked at the machines by the wall automatically, but he wasn't hooked up to any of them, and he was still and unbreathing. She didn't pause to check for a pulse, because the defibrillator had spooled up again. She set the pads back onto Becket's bare skin and called, "Clear!" once again as she pushed the control button.

He jerked again, but went limp and unresponsive once more. Vivian's vision was blurry as she put the paddles in place for a third time, but she saw Tara out of the corner of her eye and paused. "Clear..." she said hopelessly. "Tara, don't touch..."

"He's going to be okay!" Tara said tearfully. "He's going to be okay!"

Vivian thought it was only her vision swimming with tears and then realized that Becket's chest really was moving again, the faintest sign of his chest rising and falling. She dropped the paddles and groped for a pulse at his throat.

His heart was beating, thready and uncertain under her fingertips, but there. He was breathing.

He was alive, and destiny be damned.

CHAPTER 40

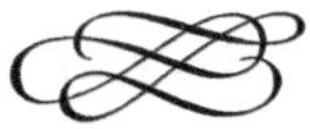

Someone was calling for a bucket and they were being really loud about it. Did someone need to throw up? Becket felt kind of queasy, like he'd been on a boat for a long time and solid land was swaying underneath him.

That was when he woke up enough to realize that it was his own name he was hearing.

"Becket, Becket?"

It was Vivian, and she sounded like she was crying. She was crying because he was going to die and leave her and it wasn't fair to put her and her kids through that.

But wait?

He *wasn't* dead.

We were, his unicorn said, as puzzled and dazed as Becket himself was. *We **were.***

Becket wasn't sure what had happened, or where he was, but he wasn't dead.

What happened? He tried to ask the question out loud, but he couldn't quite make his mouth work yet.

"He's alive?" It was David's voice and Becket wondered if he'd managed to save Timothy, or if his own miraculous yank from the brink of death had been at the cost of the boy's. Had he reserved some necessary energy to save himself? Everything was hazy and disconnected.

"Barely," Vivian said sharply. "Hand me that saturation monitor—no, the white pinchy thing on the cord. *Look where I'm pointing!*"

"He's not moving," David's voice said skeptically. There was a rattle of equipment rolling across the carpet.

Becket felt something squeeze a finger.

"He flat-lined," Vivian said briskly. "It's not like the movies where he's going to get up and start dancing around two minutes after his heart is restarted. Tara, honey, don't let the puppy chew on those cords."

He'd died. He'd died but he wasn't dead. *What does this mean?* he asked his unicorn.

It was a knot in the string of our life, his unicorn observed in wonder. *It was this. I could not see past it.*

How far does it go? Was this only a temporary respite? Was he only prolonging Vivian's inevitable heartache? His chest hurt wickedly.

He could feel his unicorn puzzling through the future possibilities. *I...don't know.*

That wasn't the confidence that Becket usually encountered. *You can't see it?*

There are too many choices, his unicorn said in wonder. *The string past the knot has frayed into a hundred strands. There is no single destiny.*

Some kinds of destiny were good, Becket remembered, achingly. Did this mean that Vivian wasn't his mate anymore? Could you only have the good parts of fate if you took the bad?

No, his unicorn scoffed. *It doesn't mean that at all. Stop being so dramatic. All of the choices lead to her.*

Becket felt a wave of relief. He could not imagine living anymore if it was without Vivian.

She was back now, leaning over him to peel up his eyelids and shine a light to stab him in the brain.

"Vivian," he said, forcing his mouth to move this time.

"Becket, you son of a bitch. If you ever try to sacrifice yourself like that again in front of my children, I will murder you myself."

"Language," Becket teased her breathlessly.

She dropped a kiss on his forehead. "They've heard worse. Tara is covering the dog's ears."

"The dog still doesn't have a name," Becket pointed out. "He really should, by now."

Vivian rested her forehead against his. "He's lucky," she said gently.

"I'm lucky," Becket said. He felt incredibly high and exhausted. She must have given him epinephrine, because he felt ready to vibrate out of his skin. But he was *alive*.

"No," Vivian corrected him. "The dog. His name is Lucky."

CHAPTER 41

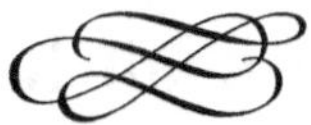

avid paid for a private plane, and a repair on the lock of Vivian's door, and he took care of the police report that Vivian's neighbor had filed when it was obvious that she'd been broken into and a car was abandoned on their lawn, all before they even got home.

Vivian suspected that David would have done much more for them, if she'd pressed the issue, given them some of his buckets of money, or bought them a new house. But by the time that Timothy was waking from his coma and Becket was recovering his energy, Vivian only wanted to go home and be in her quiet, unmagical neighborhood again pretending everything was normal.

It certainly felt normal, juggling Shane in his car seat and trying to herd Tara inside after the limo from the airport dropped them off. Becket, basically recovered now, was carrying the puppy and bulging bags of their things; David had insisted that they take it all home with them and the driver was carrying the box of diapers and another several bags. Vivian was already dreading trying to find space for all of it.

She used the new key in the new lock and found the old house, exactly as they'd left it, in homey disarray.

It was late, and she and Becket fell directly into getting everyone to bed.

"I'm hungry," Tara protested, although she'd eaten dinner and a dozen cookies on the plane.

Vivian opened the fridge with trepidation and found that nothing had spoiled in the few days they were gone.

Had it really only been a few days?

So much had happened.

So much had changed.

She gave Tara a cheese stick, which was painstakingly shredded into a dozen feathery pieces and slowly eaten. She got almost everything unpacked while Tara tried to talk around her strings of cheese about her new doll and her puppy and other children at Tiny Paws in a droning, mumbling monologue that Vivian didn't even try to follow.

Becket got Shane changed and dressed for bed, then took over making conversational noises at Tara and encouraging her to eat the food instead of playing with it, while Vivian took Shane to nurse before bed.

He was asleep after only a brief suckle and Vivian lay him down in his crib and finally had a moment to pause and remind herself that they were safe now, home again, and that Becket wasn't dying.

Becket wasn't dying.

Vivian hadn't had time to process that yet, and she still wasn't sure how much she really believed it.

She'd spent their entire relationship braced for it, ready for it, telling herself that she was strong enough to do this again, and now that the weight was off their shoulders, she felt brittle and undone.

She felt the tears sting behind her eyes and she looked down at Shane, limp and akimbo in his crib and wondered how anyone in the world was strong enough to live knowing death was at the end of every path.

Concentrating on her breath drew Vivian back to steady, and she wound up the musical mobile and turned off the overhead light, closing the door quietly behind her.

Becket had prodded Tara through her cheese stick and gotten her to the bathroom to brush her teeth.

"I tried telling her she didn't have to brush them tonight," Becket said with a shrug. "It seems like a special occasion."

"You won't be able to convince her," Vivian said from ample experience. "'The 'dennis' says so.'"

"She is a very determined little girl," Becket said with admiration.

"Someday, I will appreciate that," Vivian said. "Or at least, that's what I tell myself to get through these days."

"You will definitely appreciate it someday," Becket said.

"Do you...*know* that?" Vivian had been dying to ask how much he still knew about the future.

Becket lowered his voice, glancing towards the bathroom where Tara was painstakingly polishing each tooth, talking about every one of them as she went. "I've never been able to see anyone else's future, only what I do and touch. It makes me a poor soothsayer. It's almost like the future I saw before ended in a great knot, with only one possible end, and now I'm past that and it's frayed into so many strands. I can't say for certain what's going to happen, how anything will end up."

"And your magic?"

"It feels empty," Becket said quietly, thoughtfully. "But not gone. Like a well that will refill after it's sat for a while. I'm still drained from saving Timothy, but I think it will come back."

"And it won't...cost you?"

"I think it will be like any magic, any form of energy. I'll be able to run myself dry if I'm not careful, but using it won't harm me irreparably. I'll have to experiment."

"Carefully," Vivian said fiercely. "With me there to slap you out of it if necessary."

"You brought me back once," Becket said. "I'm sure you could again."

"I don't want to have to," Vivian said. "I lost you once..."

Then he was drawing her into his arms and she was trying very hard not to cry into his wonderful chest.

Tara came out of the bathroom and found them this way. She wrapped her arms as far around their legs as she could. "Double hug!" she cried.

"Double hug," Vivian said, dashing her tears away. "Are you ready for bed?"

Tara looked up appraisingly. "I'm still hungry," she said.

"You just had a cheese stick," Becket pointed out.

"I'm thirsty," Tara said triumphantly.

"You had a drink in the bathroom," Vivian reminded her.

"I have to—"

"Do you want to sleep with Lucky?" Vivian said desperately.

Tara's eyes got very big and hopeful and she nodded in wordless excitement and ran to get dressed for bed.

Lucky was as delighted as she was by this arrangement, and Vivian was pretty sure that neither of them would sleep immediately. She hoped that the bedding and pillow would both survive the night.

When she was pulling the door shut behind her, Tara called, "The puppy is hungry!"

"He already had dinner," Vivian countered.

"The puppy is thirsty!" Tara attempted.

"You don't want the puppy to come to bed after drinking and get it wet!"

"The puppy—"

"Goodnight, Tara."

She left the door cracked so that Lucky could get out without waking Tara.

"I don't know how I did this without you," Vivian confessed, when she met Becket again on the couch after everyone was quiet.

He put his phone down and drew her down beside him, kissing her forehead as they leaned into each other and drank in the moment of peace and quiet.

The forehead kiss turned into a deep, hungry kiss on her lips, which moved into a journey down her neck.

All of Vivian's need for sleep washed away into another kind of need and she slipped her shirt off over her head and tugged at Becket's. He helped her get it off with the barest break in kissing her, and they made love right there on the couch, desperate for the affirmation that they were both still living.

CHAPTER 42

The morning routine felt very odd the next day…and absolutely, perfectly right.

Becket took the puppy out with Tara in the morning while Vivian drowsed on the couch with a cup of coffee as she nursed Shane, and then he made them all breakfast and got everyone dressed and out the door.

Crystal greeted them at the clinic with great alarm.

"What happened?! Your text said you were in Denver? There was a report of a home invasion in your neighborhood. Was that *your* house? Were you *there?*"

Vivian very calmly explained that it had only

been a misunderstanding, and that everything was fine and no one had been hurt, and it wasn't nearly as dramatic as it all sounded.

Crystal, barely appeased, sent Vivian to the first appointment and Becket got a cup of coffee in the break room while she got the patient checked in and took vitals.

He was pouring the fragrant brew into his cup and wishing he'd taken the time to make cookies, when he abruptly realized that he didn't plan to leave in the spring. When had he made the decision? he wondered.

Maybe when he'd come back to life and realized he had things worth living for.

This was the place for him, both the clinic and the sleepy town full of shifters. It was a place where he could do good. He could use his gifts now, if he was careful. It wouldn't be like it was when he was young, showy and self-serving, but if he could quietly help his patients, they might never even know what he was doing. Minor corrections here, subtle healing there, just enough to fix the problems without crossing over into *unexplained miracle* territory.

The clinic could become a place where shifter children could safely be treated without undue questions.

And at night, he could go home to Vivian and her children and Lucky.

Becket was honestly not sure what part of that potential future he loved the most. Healing without reservations and sacrifice? Helping to raise Tara and Shane? Hot nights with Vivian? Would she want more kids? More pets?

Roots, his unicorn sighed happily. *Home. Foals.*

He'd never dared to think about having a child of his own, because he'd never seen a life long enough to commit to one. He adored Tara and Shane enough that he thought he would be satisfied with them, but vasectomies were reversible, if she was game! He'd have to ask Vivian some questions.

Questions about their future.

He had a future.

They had a future.

When he passed Vivian in the hallway later, he didn't hesitate to kiss her.

"We're at *work*!" she giggled, glancing down the hall. "We have to be professional."

"What are they going to do, fire me?" Becket challenged. "I'm about to sign a long-term contract with the clinic."

Vivian's eyes lit up. "You mean…"

"There's no reason I can't, now. Jamison has been begging me to."

This time, she kissed him, not even checking first to see if anyone was watching.

Becket floated through the rest of the day, not minding the kids who were cranky or the parents who were impatient.

He had a future.

They had a future.

And it was beautiful.

CHAPTER 43

The house in the Chicago suburbs was gorgeous and tall, tucked just off a quiet road with a long driveway and a brick arch. The lawn was winter-dead and the trees were bare, but it still had that landscaped look that Vivian's house would never have, besides being twice the size and elegance. There was a tasteful string of white Christmas lights along the fence.

Vivian wanted to turn around and flee.

What was she doing here? Why did she think this was a good idea?

Tara tugged on her hand. "Mommy, Mommy, are we going to go in? I'm cold." They were standing at the end of a concrete walk to the front door, while Becket unloaded their bags from the taxi. Shane's car seat was already cutting off the circulation on Vivian's other arm.

Vivian drew in her breath. "We're going to go in," she said valiantly. "Do you have your bag?"

It couldn't possibly be as terrible as she was imagining it would be. She'd already explained that she was coming with a new boyfriend, as awkward as that was, and Jin's baby. A baby that she'd kept a secret for too long already. She'd said it as a challenge, expecting the invitation to be rescinded, and Jin's mother had been quiet for a long moment on the phone.

Then she had insisted that Vivian bring them all, and Vivian still wasn't sure if it was out of an abundance of politeness or a sense of honor, but she hadn't been able to say no, and with the insurance check that had finally been cut, she couldn't even protest that they couldn't afford the trip.

So here they were, after a grueling flight, facing one of Vivian's greatest fears.

Vivian took her hand back from Tara to grip the handle of her rolling suitcase. "Get your bag, darling." The door to the house opened and Tara went into her timid mode as Becket, with the lion's share of the luggage, came up behind her.

"You got this," he murmured quietly, and it gave Vivian the strength to start walking.

Jin's mother fluttered in the doorway, and his father stood immovably beside her as Vivian made the agonizing trip up the sidewalk. Tara trailed behind her so close that she tread on her heels. Was the little girl picking up on the stress that Vivian could feel shedding from her like needles from a neglected Christmas tree in January, or was it just her natural reserve?

The distance between them got shorter as Vivian held her breath, and then, after an awkward pause, Jin's father stepped forward with an extended hand. "Let me help you with that."

There was a flurry of greetings and gratitude. They insisted that they were called Sue and Tom, not Mrs. and Mr. Yang. Becket was a perfect gentleman and Tara caught sight of the Christmas tree inside and forgot to be shy, just as Shane woke up and gave a wail for attention.

Jin's mother took them upstairs to a pair of bedrooms, with a toddler bed for Tara clad in a pink quilt and a crib for Shane that was so new that it still smelled like fresh paint. Tara greeted her bed and the stuffies and pillows that covered it with a crow of delight. Becket and Vivian exchanged a sheepish, blushing look over the double bed in the room they were clearly meant to share. They left their luggage in the bedrooms and tramped noisily back downstairs. Vivian was sure that the house, with its white carpet and perfect order, was probably usually silent, but there was no keeping Tara and Shane perfectly quiet, and the Yangs didn't seem to expect them to.

"We have food," Sue said eagerly, and she ushered them into the dining room, where a long table groaned under a spread of American snacks and Chinese treats.

Tara stared in wonder, and to Vivian's relief, seemed eager to try various things. Shane, sleepy from the trip, clung to Vivian at first, then was happy enough to pass off, first to Sue and then to Tom, who each took turns cooing over him and laughing at his giggles and faces. They talked about the trip, and about Tara's school, and Vivian's work at the clinic, which seamlessly included Becket, and they spoke easily about holiday memories and favorite foods as Tara nibbled dumplings and declared them delicious before giving the rest to Vivian.

Jin came up in the conversation without effort or awkwardness, and Vivian was eager to hear their stories about his childhood. Becket held his own, adding his personal tales where they were relevant, and the Yangs were kind and inclusive with him. Vivian thought that the moment of shifter recognition that he'd shared with Tom when they met was helpful.

Her worries that Jin's parents would be interested in Shane to the neglect of Tara was swiftly dispelled when Tom handed Tara a tiny white plush cat with one paw lifted. "It's lucky," he explained.

"I'm lucky, too," Tara said softly, and they exchanged a knowing smile. Shortly after, they disappeared together into the fenced back yard.

"Tara is a kirin?" Sue asked wistfully.

Becket had taken Shane to change him and Vivian was helping Sue put food back in the fridge.

Vivian nodded. "Yes, and she's very good at shifting and knows when she shouldn't. I was hoping you could help her understand a little more about…what she is. Jin didn't tell me much. Before."

"Tom knew she would be," Jin's mother said gladly. "He's been looking forward to teaching her. And Shane?"

"Nothing yet, as far as I know," Vivian said.

Becket told her that he'd know if the baby was close to shifting, but that there was no way of guessing if a child would be a shifter or not until they got to that point. Would they be disappointed if he wasn't a kirin as well?

"Thank you so much for bringing them." For the first time, tears sprang to her eyes. "They're all we have left of him."

"Oh, I should have brought them much sooner," Vivian said, fighting back her own tears. "It's been…hard."

"You've done so well!"

They were sobbing on each other when Becket returned with Shane, who babbled happily. "Let's go look at the Christmas tree," he suggested, backing from the room.

"No, no," Sue said. "Come, James Becket, come and be part of our family and carry on with us."

If Becket found it uncomfortable to have Sue hug him and pat his back and cry a little on his stomach, he gave no sign of it. He hugged her back. "I could never replace him," he said sincerely.

"Of course not," Sue said practically. "But you can share his place in our hearts."

"Mama, Mommy!" Tara came running back in,

red-cheeked, with Tom more sedately behind her. "I can fly!"

"Fly?" Vivian asked in alarm, meeting Tom's eyes. "Should I be worried?"

"It's not really flying," Tom explained serenely. "I only showed her how to walk above things, so the grass blades don't bend. It's just floating a little."

"I have to tell Teacher Addy so she can put it in my book!" Tara crowed. "Where is the food?"

Sue was happy to take her to the kitchen for snacks, despite Vivian's warnings that she would probably not want dinner if she ate again now.

"Grandmothers are supposed to indulge their grandchildren," she said merrily. "This is my job!"

Becket gave Shane to Tom when he gave the merest indication that he'd like to hold him again, and though Shane was reluctant to switch from Becket's arms at first, he quickly cheered to his grandfather's goofy expressions and careful bouncing. "Shall we go look at the Christmas tree, young man?"

Vivian marveled that she had ever thought that Jin's parents were cold and disapproving. Was it only her own fears that had colored her impressions of them? Was it Jin's desire for independence? She felt limp with relief and warm from their welcome. They had included Becket without question and not given her a moment of grief for keeping Shane a secret or avoiding them after Jin's death.

"How's it going?" Becket asked, when they were alone in the dining room and he could gather her up into his arms. "Better than you feared?"

"Everything is fine," she said, leaning into his collar and feeling the comfort of him flow through her like warmth from a fire. "Everything is *perfect.*"

And for that instant, at least, everything was. Her family had expanded again, and they were safe and happy and whole.

"It's...kind of weird timing, here in your in-laws house at Christmas," Becket said, backing away from her at last. "But I've been thinking about this for a long time, and I don't want to put it off any more. I don't want to put anything off, ever."

Vivian couldn't help the smile that was spreading over her face. "You're asking me to marry you, aren't you?"

His smile matched hers, helpless and happy. "I'm sorry, it's not quite the perfect moment that I should have planned out. I don't have the ring yet.

I didn't write a speech. I just know that I want to be with you, forever, and be official for your kids—"

"Our kids," Vivian corrected. "You're family now. Sue said so."

"I never thought this was something I'd be able to do," Becket said, taking her face in his hands. "I never thought I'd have forever to promise to someone."

"We don't know if we have forever now," Vivian reminded him. "Even you can't see that future now."

"Whatever I can have with you, I want every moment of it together."

"Yes," Vivian agreed. "Yes, I'll marry you. I want every second of our forever with you."

He kissed her then, deeply and unhurried. They had a lifetime ahead to enjoy each other, a future that lay out before them like a lazy river of love and devotion.

Vivian had worried that their passion would fade without the urgency of an end date, but she was more enamored with this man than ever, and she was confident that he adored her and would, always.

"Oh, no," Vivian suddenly realized. "Do I have to change my name to Singlehorn?"

They were still laughing when Tara returned with Sue and a plate of nibbled treats. "Mommy, are you okay?"

Vivian swept her up into her arms, to Tara's mixed alarm and delight, and hugged her daughter close. "I am better than okay," she promised. "I am *alive.*"

AFTERWORD

Oh man. This was *a book* and I loved every minute that I was writing it, even when I cried. (Sometimes, writers cry because the *writing* is hard. This was only crying because the *story* was hard.) I tried very hard to balance laughter and hope and connection with the despair and give it a happy ending that made all the painful and uncertain parts completely worth it. The cute puppy helped a lot.

I am really looking forward to writing the next book in the series, Gryphon's Instinct. I can't wait to introduce you to this delightful and slightly dysfunctional family who needs just the right skeptic to waltz into town and try to debunk the rumors of magic in Nickel City.

Sending signed paperbacks from Alaska can be challenging, but I have the next best thing available—bookplates! Find them at my webpage.

If you enjoyed this book, I would very much appreciate your reviews on Amazon, Goodreads, or Bookbub (follow me at any of the above) if you enjoyed this book! I love to hear from readers, and you are welcome to email me at elvaherself@elvabirch.com with any questions, or if you catch any stray typos…or if you just want to say hi.

To find out about new releases, you can follow me on Amazon, subscribe to my newsletter, or like me on Facebook. You are also welcome to join my Reader's Retreat on Facebook for sneak previews, cut scenes, giveaways, and more—including the book I'm not writing!

I also write under other pen names—keep reading for information about my other available titles!

~Elva

MORE BY ELVA BIRCH

Want some more extra short stories, including a Shifting Sands Resort ménage? Join my mailing list for sneak previews, extras, bonus stories, and more, or join my Reader's Retreat on Facebook!

* * *

A Day Care for Shifters: A hot new full-length series about adorable shifter kids and their struggling single parents in a town full of mystery and surprise. Start the series with Wolf's Instinct, when Addison comes to Nickel City to take a job at a very special day care and finds a family to belong to. A gentle ice-cream-straight-from-the-container escape. Sweet and sizzling!

* * *

Get a free Day Care for Shifters short story from baby Ryan's point of view, First Christmas, at my webpage!

Want some more extra short stories, including a Shifting Sands Resort ménage? Join my mailing list for sneak previews, extras, bonus stories, and more, or join my Reader's Retreat on Facebook!

* * *

The Royal Dragons of Alaska: A fascinating alternate world where Alaska is ruled by secret dragon shifters. Adventure, romance, and humor! Reluctant royalty, relentless enemies...dogs, camping, and magic! Start with The Dragon Prince of Alaska.

* * *

Suddenly Shifters: A hilarious series of novellas, serials, and shorts set in the small town of Anders Canyon, where something (in the water?) is making ordinary citizens turn into shifters. Start with Something in the Water!

* * *

Lawn Ornament Shifters: The series that was only supposed to be a joke, this is a collection of short, ridiculous romances featuring unusual shifters, myths, and magic. Cross-your-legs funny and full of heart! Start with The Flamingo's Fated Mate!

* * *

Birch Hearts: An enchanting collection of short stories and novellas. Unconstrained by theme or setting, each short read has romance, magic, and heart, with a satisfying conclusion. And always, the impossible and irresistible. Start with a sampler plate in Prompted 2 for fourteen pieces of sweet-to-sizzling flash fiction, or dive in with the novella, Better Half - which you can get free for joining my mailing list!

Shifting Sands Resort: A complete ten-book series - plus two collections of shorts. This is a sizzling shifter romance set at a tropical island resort. Each book stands alone but connects into a great mystery with a thrilling conclusion. Start with Tropical Tiger Spy or dive in to the Omnibus edition, with all of the novels, short stories, and novellas in my preferred reading order! This series crosses over with Fire and Rescue Shifters and Shifter Kingdom.

* * *

Fae Shifter Knights: A complete four-book fantasy portal romp, with cute pets and swoon-worthy knights stuck in a world of wonders like refrigerators and ham sandwiches. Start with Dragon of Glass!

* * *

Green Valley Shifters: A sweet, small town series with single dads, secret shifters, sweet kids, and spinsters. Low-peril and steamy! Standalone books where you can revisit your favorite characters. Start with Dancing Barefoot! Green Valley crosses over with **Virtue Shifters**. Sexy and funny, each book set in the little town of Virtue promises a heartwarming story, a touch of fate, and a little bit of adventure. Start with Timber Wolf!

BEHIND THE SCENES

What is Patreon?

Patreon is a site where readers and fans can support creators with monthly subscriptions.

At my Patreon, I have tiers with early rough drafts of my books, flash fiction, coloring pages, signed and sketched paperbacks, exclusive swag, original artwork, photographs…and so much more! Every month is a little different, and there is a price for every budget. Patreon allows me to do projects that aren't very commercial and makes my income stream a little less unpredictable. It also gives me a place to connect with my fans!

Come find out what's going on behind the scenes and keep me creating at Patreon! patreon.com/ellenmillion

Carina Andresen surged to her feet, sweeping her camp chair out from under her as a make-shift weapon.

Wolf! her brain hammered at her. *Wolf!* She was going to become an Alaska tourist statistic and get eaten by a wolf on her second week in the kingdom.

Logic slowly caught up with her panic.

The animal across the campfire from her was smaller and *doggier* than a wolf, and it was only a moment before Carina could get her breath and heartbeat back under control and recognize that it was well-groomed, shyly eyeing her sizzling hot dog, and wagging its tail.

Alaska probably had stray dogs, too; she wasn't *that* far from civilization.

"Hi there, sweetie," Carina said, her voice still unnaturally high as she put her chair back on its legs. "Does that smell good? Want a bit of hot dog?" Carina turned the hot dog in the flame and waggled it suggestively.

The non-edible dog sped up his tail and when Carina broke off a piece of the meat and dropped it beside her, he crept around the fire and slurped it eagerly up off the ground.

The second bite he took gently from her fingers, and by the second hot dog she dared to pet him.

Within about thirty minutes and five hot dogs, he was leaning on her and letting her scratch his ears and neck as he wagged his tail and groaned in delight.

"Oh, you're just a dear," Carina said. "I bet someone's missing you." He was a husky mix, Carina guessed; he was tall and strong, with a long, thick coat of dark gray fur and white feet. His ears were upright, and his tail was long and feathered. He didn't have a collar, but he was clearly friendly. "You want some water?"

The dog licked his lips as if he had understood, and Carina carefully stood so she didn't frighten him.

But he seemed to be past any shyness now, and he followed Carina to her van trustingly, tail waving happily. He drank the offered water from a frying pan, and then tried to give Carina a kiss dripping with slobber.

"You probably already have a name," Carina said, laughingly trying to escape the wet tongue. "But I'm going to call you Shadow for now." She had a grubby towel hanging from her clothesline and used it to dry off his face. They played a gentle game of tug-of-war, testing each other's strength and manners.

Shadow seemed to approve of his new name and gave her a canine grin once she'd won the towel back from him.

"Alright, Shadow, let's go collect some more firewood."

The area was rich with downed wood to harvest, and with the assistance of a folding hand saw, Carina was able to find several heaping armloads of solid, dry wood, enough to keep a cheerful fire going for a few days if she was frugal. It was comforting to have Shadow around for the task; she wasn't quite as nervous about the noises she heard, and he was a happy distraction from her own brain.

He frolicked with her, and found a stick three times his own length to drag around possessively.

"So helpful!" Carina laughed at him, as he knocked over an empty pot and swiped her across the knees so that she nearly fell.

When she sat down beside the crackling fire in her low camp chair, Shadow abandoned his prize stick and crowded close to lay his head on her knee. Carina petted him absently.

"Someone's looking for you, you big softy," she said regretfully. She would have to try to reunite the dog with his owner but, for now, it was nice having a companion around the camp.

Of all the things she expected when she went running for the wilderness, she had never guessed that the silence would be the worst. She had been camping plenty, but it was always *with* someone. Since their parents had died, that someone was usually her sister, June, but some-times it was a friend or a roommate. She was used to having someone to point out birds and animals to, someone to share chores with, stretch out tarps with. When it was just her, the spaces seemed vaster, the wind bit harder, and even the birds were less cheerful.

"You probably don't care about the birds that would make my life list," she told Shadow mournfully.

Shadow wagged his tail in a rustle of leaves.

She didn't have her life list anymore to add to anyway. Everything had been left behind: her phone, her computer, her identity. Her entire life was on hold. She had the van to live in, some sup-plies and a small nest egg to start from, so she ought to be able to stay out of sight long enough to regroup and...she didn't know what to do from here. Find a journalist willing to take her story and clear her name?

To fill the quiet, and to help ignore the ache in her chest, she read aloud from the brochure on Alaska that she had been given at the border sta-tion. She'd found it that evening while she was emptying the glovebox to take stock of supplies, and Shadow seemed as good a listener as any.

"Like many modern monarchies, Alaska has an

elected council of officials who do most of the day to day rulings of this vast, rich land. The royal family is steeped in tradition and mystery, and holds many veto powers, as well as acting as ambassadors to other countries. Known as the Dragon King, the Alaskan sovereign is a reserved figure who rarely appears in public. Margaret, the Queen of Alaska, died twelve years ago, leaving behind six sons." There was a photo, with boys ranging from about seven to maybe twenty-five. Two of the middle children were identical. One of the twins was wearing a hockey jersey and grinning, the other wore glasses and looked annoyed. The oldest —or at least the tallest—was frowning seriously at the others. The only blonde of the bunch was one of the middle boys, who was looking intently at the camera. The youngest looked painfully bored. They all had tongue-twisting names of more syllables than Carina wanted to try pronouncing.

Carina thought it was an interesting photo. The tension between the oldest two was palpable, and the they were all dressed surprisingly casually. She didn't follow royal gossip much beyond scanning headlines at grocery store checkouts, but Alaska never seemed to make waves; they were rarely involved in dramas and scandals.

Shadow raised his head and cocked his head at some imagined noise in the forest.

"That's a lot of siblings," Carina observed, ruffling his ears. She felt so much safer having him beside her. "Just one sister was more than enough for me." She didn't want to admit how much she missed that sister right now.

Shadow returned his head to her knee. "Alaska is a member of the Small Kingdoms Alliance, an exclusive collective of independent monarchies scattered throughout the world. Although Alaska has large amounts of land, they qualify for membership because of their small population."

Carina turned the brochure over. "There are hot springs about fifty miles north of Fairbanks! I hope to make it there." *Before* she ran out of cash. It looked expensive. Maybe she could get work there...she'd heard that it wasn't hard to find under-the-table jobs in this country.

Shadow suddenly leapt to his feet, barking at something crashing through the woods behind them and Carina nearly tipped over backwards in her camp chair trying to stand up.

She expected to find a moose, or possibly a bear, and she was already picking up the chair to use as a flimsy defense against a charging wild animal.

But it was only a man stepping out of the woods, in an official dark blue uniform emblazoned with the eight gold stars of Alaska.

For a moment, terror every bit as keen as the panic that had gripped her at the first sight of Shadow washed over her. They'd found her.

"You're trespassing on royal land and I'm going to have to ask you to leave," he said.

Then she realized with relief that it wasn't a police officer. He was only a park ranger.

* * *

...or was he? Discover love and adventure in a wonderful alternate Alaska with camping and dogs and magic. Reluctant royalty and relentless enemies! Pick up The Dragon Prince of Alaska *today!*

A PREVIEW OF TROPICAL TIGER SPY

When Amber booked her vacation at Shifting Sands Resort, she was expecting a lazy tropical vacation at a luxury escape for shifters...she wasn't expecting to meet a sexy under-cover tiger shifter spy who set her blood on fire, or to become a part of his investigation into why shifters are disappearing from the resort! An excerpt of Tropical Tiger Spy.

Amber walked meekly with the guards, trying not to be too obvious about looking around. The dog-catcher was lying unexpectedly loose at her shoulders, and when she glanced at the man holding the pole, he glared back and fingered a button on the handle. The other guard, walking behind her with the gun trained on her, cleared his throat, and Amber put her head down and continued to shamble with them. She was short, so it was easy to walk slowly and look like she was using a normal pace.

The looseness of the noose around her neck got her brain spinning.

They were expecting a mountain cat—an American mountain cat. A *big* mountain cat. If she shifted, the dog-catcher would be tight around the neck of a big cat. But around her small cat shape...

As quickly as the idea occurred to her, Amber put it in motion, shifting as she pretended to stumble.

Her clothing fell away from her cat form even as she jumped—straight through the noose—and scrambled for the wall of the mesh enclosure they were walking past. She heard the crackle of the dog-catcher rather than feeling it through her thick fur, and realized belatedly that it must be electrified. She wasn't sure if she would have made this attempt if she'd known that, but it was far too late now, and her coat, meant for cold mountain winters, had protected her from the worst of it.

She climbed in a panic, the agility of her cat form driving her, and as the guard behind her fired and missed, and missed again as she switched directions up the enclosure and reached the roof.

She heard the zoo erupt into roars and animal cries of encouragement. A human voice even cried out, "Go, kitty cat!"

"Shit!" the guards said in unison.

More wild shots followed her. Needles hissed by as Amber made it up to the roof of the enclosure. She ran and leaped to the next. She was already two cages away while the guards were still peering up onto the first. Then she switched directions entirely and leaped across the path to a new row of cages.

Her night sight let her see better than she had as a human, and her height gave her a clear view. Lights all along the wall had come on, showing her that she had no real chance of getting over them—though she could probably squeeze between the barbed wire with little damage thanks to her coat, she was too small to make it to the top of the wall to try; nothing was built up close to it. She noticed the cameras, too, now swiveling back into the enclosure to try to find her, and had a glimpse of a helicopter on one of the low roofs towards the back.

"Goddamn it, do you see it?" one guard called to the other.

"Beehag said it was a mountain cat, not a goddamn *little* cat!" the other complained.

Their voices were clear to Amber's excellent hearing.

Instead of immediate escape, Amber looked

for hiding spaces, and found one in a pile of construction materials towards the end of the zoo. While the cameras were still re-positioning to try to follow her, she dashed out of sight down the side of one of the enclosures and flattened herself to fit in a tiny space on top of a pile of rocks, under dimension lumber and roof tiles. From here, she could see a dozen more hiding places that she'd be able to make it to in short order, and she had a good vantage for seeing oncoming intruders.

She could actually see that the entire zoo was actually much more suited for containing big animals. She'd be able to get out, she felt, with her first taste of confidence as the adrenaline began to release its hold on her. She just had to lie low, and she'd be able to sneak out of the front gates when the timing was right.

"Call it in!" one of the guards was saying.

"Fuck no, you call it in," the other protested.

Eventually, they worked out who was making the call, and the little two-way radio crackled in return as they explained their mistake.

"Escaped?" Even over the poor quality radio from a distance, Amber recognized Alistair's voice, and it made the hackles on her neck rise.

The guards fell over each other to justify their

actions, and Amber gave a little cat smile to hear them describe her as basically supernatural.

There was a moment of silence in response, and then Alistair's crisp accent. "She won't get far. We've got her *mate* here."

Mate?

Amber knew without a doubt that they meant Tony, and it was everything she could do not to bolt from her hiding hole right then to find and defend him. But what did they mean by 'mate?' She could all but hear the emphasis that Alistair was putting on it.

The waiter at the resort had used the same word.

Whatever they meant by it, she knew that Alistair was right—knowing that they had Tony—that they might *hurt* Tony to get her, meant that Alistair had Amber as surely as if that noose *had* been tight around her neck.

Read the rest of *Tropical Tiger Spy* now!